The Grass Labyrinth

T0097656

A successful artist is expected to give his or her all for "the work." The linked stories in *The Grass Labyrinth* challenge the reader to determine if the work is worth the pain often visited on those who share an artist's life.

A married children's book illustrator falls in love with a photorealist refugee. Their daughter, a blocked poet, becomes infatuated with a young painter with whom she shares a palpable bond. And this young painter, dumped by his girlfriend and tired of the hustle, envisions settling down with his widowed stepmother in the house where he grew up.

Whether in a college town in Pennsylvania, a loft in Brooklyn, or a ramshackle cottage on the Carolina coast, these stories explore, over a thirty-year span, how the choices the characters make shape those they love in ways they never anticipate, down through the generations.

By turns ironic, hopeful, and wry, Charlotte Holmes paints a surprising portrait of one family's intimate struggle to find the paths that will carry them to the work they want to do, the lives they want to lead, and the people they can't help but love.

The Grass Labyrinth

stories

Charlotte Holmes

BkMk Press
University of Missouri-Kansas City

Copyright © 2016 by Charlotte Holmes

BkMk Press
University of Missouri-Kansas City
5101 Rockhill Road
Kansas City, Missouri 64110
www.umkc.edu/bkmk

Financial support for this project has been provided by the
Missouri Arts Council, a state agency.

Executive editor: Robert Stewart
Managing editor: Ben Furnish
Assistant managing editor & book design: Cynthia Beard
Cover photos: Williamson Brasfield
Cover design: Siara Berry

Visit www.newletters.org/bkmk-books/the-grass-labyrinth-stories for
discussion questions and more information about this book.

BkMk Press wishes to thank Siara Berry, Morgan Hudson,
Marie Mayhugh, Brittany Green.

Library of Congress Cataloging-in-Publication Data

Names: Holmes, Charlotte, author.
Title: The grass labyrinth : stories / by Charlotte Holmes.
Description: Kansas City, MO : BkMk Press, University of Missouri-
Kansas City, [2016]
Identifiers: LCCN 2015046575 | ISBN 9781943491049 (alk. paper)
Classification: LCC PS3558.O3583 G73 2016 | DDC 813/.54--dc23
LC record available at http://lccn.loc.gov/2015046575

ISBN 978-1-943491-04-9

First edition.
Printed in the United States of America.

For Jim and Will

Acknowledgments

These stories previously appeared, sometimes in slightly different form, in the following journals: "Coast," "What Is," "Erratics," and "Taken" in *Epoch*, "The Grass Labyrinth" in *Narrative*, "Songs Without Words" and "Agnes Landowska: Her Art and Life" in *New Letters*, and "After" in *Superstition Review*. My thanks to the editors.

"Coast" was selected by Madison Smartt Bell to appear in *New Stories From the South: The Year's Best 2010*.

My thanks as well to the Millay Colony for the Arts and the D.H. Lawrence Foundation for residencies that provided time to work on these stories, the Pennsylvania Council on the Arts for fellowships, and the American-Scandinavian Foundation for a travel grant.

And thank you, thank you, thank you to my friends who read these stories, and this book, in manuscript and gave generously of their advice, encouragement, and patience: Robin Becker, Jim Brasfield, Will Brasfield, Carri Hendricks, Elizabeth Kadetsky, Judith Kalina, and Phil Whitman.

Contents

We live in two landscapes, as Augustine might have said,

One that's eternal and divine,
                          and one that's just the back yard,

—Charles Wright

Coast

According to Agnes, I've missed a lot, and she's put reading Rilke at the top of her list. I've built up the fire, and the smell of wood smoke is beginning to overtake the salt smell of the old room, and the warmth makes a dent in the dampness. Settled on one of the saggy, slip-covered sofas that have been here since my childhood, I open the worn clothbound volume, my first thought not about the poems but how her hands looked emerging from the cuffs of her black sweater, the long fingers with short-clipped nails pale against the gray linen as she handed the book to me.

"You speak German?" I asked as we sat drinking tea in her apartment last Thursday, and she said, "Henry, of course. We all learned German. And if I hadn't left, I'd speak Russian, too. Where I come from, adaptation's the name of the game."

She read the poem in Rilke's language, which I remembered a little from high school, though I didn't let on. I was too busy noticing that in her mouth, German wasn't guttural, was nearly as sibilant as the English translation she read next. She speaks English with hardly an accent—a result, she says, of leaving Poland when she was still young. Fifteen—already half her life ago.

I flip through the book, and when I find the poem, read it silently, then speak the words:

Who has no house now, will never build one.
Who is alone now, will long remain so,

From the other room, Lisa calls out, "What?"

When I don't answer, she sighs, and I hear her feet hit the floor. I can feel her standing behind me, across the room at the bedroom door. "Henry, did you say something to me?"

"No, love," I tell her, turning the page, letting my fingers graze the paper as gently as I'd touch Agnes's skin.

Lisa says, "This house is freezing," and comes to stand with her back to the fire.

"Surprising it gets so cold down here," I say.

"You'd think they'd have put in a furnace," Lisa says, fanning her hands out behind her. "Jesus, didn't your aunt ever stay here in the winter?"

I shrug, look back at the book, hoping she'll see she's interrupting me. "Aunt Lou and Caroline were tough old birds. Maybe they liked the cold."

"Like you," she says.

"Like me," I agree.

She shivers and rubs her arms. "This house is freezing," she says again.

When my mother's aunt Louise died and left her beach cottage to me, I felt the weight of stepping into a fantasy. Aunt Lou had known Jasper Johns when he lived down here, and evidently imagined me sliding easily into a life like his— a painter living cheaply in a remote Southern beach town, with few distractions.

I could (and did) make a long list of what she didn't take into account, and item #1 was that I was twenty-five and still in art school, with no means of supporting myself here, unless I wanted to work a shrimp boat. Miffed at being passed over as Lou's heir, my mother said maybe someday I'd appreciate owning a piece of oceanfront property. I guess I already do. Renting out the place from April until October allows me to just about break even with taxes and the considerable, necessary, endless repairs.

When Lisa turns to toast her front side, I say, "You can bring your book in here if you want to."

She looks back over her shoulder. "But you're in here," she says, "and I'm still angry with you."

Something small this time, a misunderstanding about dinner. I've never known Lisa to cook a main course more complicated than spaghetti, but last week she mentioned that she wanted to make Thanksgiving dinner. Not help to make it, but make it herself. It registered with me briefly, but before we left Philadelphia yesterday,

I was the one who went out and bought the hen, packed the cooler, made sure we brought along what dinner required.

This morning we slept late, as we always do after the long drive. After breakfast, she went in to take a shower. Because she'd said nothing about cooking the dinner since last week, I made the pumpkin pie, put it in the narrow, inaccurate, old oven to cook, and pulled the chicken out of the refrigerator. Lisa was out of the shower by then. I could hear her opening and closing dresser drawers in the bedroom, hear hangers moving in the closet. I went ahead and swabbed the roasting hen with olive oil and sprinkled it with sage, and made the cornbread dressing. I poured myself another cup of coffee and stood out on the front porch for a while, breathing in the smell of the ocean. I made a few rough sketches in my journal. I went for a short walk. When I came back inside, the house smelled of pumpkin pie, and Lisa was lying on the bed, reading. I figured she'd forgotten her offer to make dinner, but around three o'clock, I was just sliding the pan of chicken and dressing into the oven when she stalked into the kitchen and asked me what I thought I was doing.

Not, *What are you doing?*—which she could see, but *What do you think you're doing?*—an entirely different question, the kind my mother used to ask.

I reset the oven temperature before I answered. "Obviously, I'm making dinner."

After being with her for so long, I know the routine: a spray of words, a slammed door, an hour or two of tense silence. But this time, she altered the performance. Tears began sliding down her cheeks. Surprised, I opened my mouth, ready to apologize, but she said, "You think I'm incompetent," not a question but a statement of fact.

If I'd been thinking faster, I'd have reminded her that she doesn't enjoy cooking, and I do, and that's always the way it's been. Before I had a chance to speak, she stomped off into the bedroom, closing the door behind her, hard.

Sometimes I wonder if the human tendency is to freeze in place at whatever age we are when we meet. My father sometimes still talks to me as if I'm his boy, though I'm thirty and married eight years. And the only way I can see that Lisa's responses have changed in the twelve years I've known her is that she's more comfortable making them. If we met now, perhaps we'd treat each other differently—we'd be kinder, more reasonable. We might act like the adults that other people see functioning in the world, instead of the college freshmen we seem to become when we're together.

"Well, do what you want," I tell her now, yawning to show I don't care what she does. "You can sit over there," I nod at the couch opposite, "and pretend I'm not here." I look back at the poem, and though I haven't finished reading it, turn the page.

She starts off into the bedroom to get her book, muttering, "You're not here. You're not here. You're not here."

Sometimes, it's like living with a child.

The tide's coming in dark gray and churning, the rain moving in sheets across the water. Not much stands between me and the ocean—windows and French doors shut tight against the sea wind, the broad screened porch that embraces the house on three sides, and then a short plank walk down to a beach that erodes a few feet more each year.

Lisa used to insist that it was all a matter of perception—that I thought even the beach was grander in childhood. But the one time she said this in front of my mother, Mom backed me up. Exhaling cigarette smoke, gazing out at the water with melancholy affection, she said, "Lisa, honey, from what I recall, you were never here when Henry was a child." And for once, my wife didn't have a come-back.

Now she plops down on the sofa across from me, and drops a couple of heavy tomes on the coffee table between us. For four years, Lisa taught middle-school English while I worked on my MFA at Tyler and then got a job as a medical illustrator. As soon as we could swing it financially, she went back to school, earned an MA in literature, and now she's studying for her PhD comps. Pale and small, she's developed muscles from hauling around these library volumes. She draws her legs up under her and wraps herself in the afghan, pulls one of the books onto her lap, and rubs her forehead.

"Jesus," she says. "I'm so tired." She used to complain that teaching adolescents exhausted her, that after a day at school, she had no energy left to read. Now she reads all the time and she still complains about being tired. She opens the book where her marker is, but after a few minutes I look up and she's staring across the room into the fire.

"Try driving for ten hours in a rainstorm," I almost say, but realize she'd only argue that she offered to drive half the distance before we'd even left Philadelphia. And then I'd feel compelled to point out that had she driven us, the ten-hour drive would have stretched to twelve. And lifting her chin, she'd say, "I drive the speed limit," enhancing her reason with an implied rebuke.

That argument played out, I look down into the open pages of my book and think about Agnes, spending Thanksgiving with her husband in a city hundreds of miles from here. Even though she says her husband barely knows how to boil water, I put him in the kitchen, allow Agnes to be in her studio, with the gray light from the window falling across her strong-boned face, strands of dark hair trailing down her neck from the bun that's always unraveling. I think about her hands moving swiftly among the jars and brushes and tubes, mixing colors, and the smell of turpentine in the room. It clings to her, so when I bury my face in her hair, it's what I breathe in, along with a faint smell I couldn't place until I used the bar of soap in her bathroom.

Because she lives in New York, two hours from Philly by train, I've been able to see her only a few times in the two months since we met. What I know of her life I've mostly collaged from scraps that form, I know, an incomplete picture. Once I asked her, "Where did you buy that sweater?" just so I could imagine her buying it.

She looked at me, confused, and said, "I didn't buy it. I made it. Why?" but instead of the real reason, I said, "I like the color."

She looked down at it. "It's black," she said, and raised an eyebrow at me.

"I like the color on you, is what I meant," I told her, and she thanked me.

Our time together is too compressed to allow for the boring interludes where details of life fall in. Maybe that's why she's the one I want to turn to and say, "Do you hear that?" as the ocean pounds against the sand. I'd like her to smell the dampness in this musty room, so different from the smells of the usual rooms where we're together. Maybe I want to hear her say, "This reminds me of . . ." and have her fill in some blank about her life that I couldn't otherwise imagine.

Maybe what I want is just to watch her take in the details of a place I know so well, see them filter into her consciousness, and come back changed, infused with her own quirky vision.

The night we met, our breath clouded in the brittle air. She laughed and said the clouds were poems we had yet to find the words to. The next morning she woke and, before opening her eyes, laid her palm against my cheek and said my name. Last Thursday, I gripped her hands in mine as she arched above me, and I looked into her eyes and thought, *Who are you? What do you want from me?* Almost before the thought had finished forming, she leaned down and put her mouth over mine, binding me to her with the intricate threads of desire, so that who she was and what she wanted became secondary—tertiary—to the way our bodies fit together. For the first time in my life, I understood the meaning of "becoming one" with another person. That evening, standing on the platform waiting for my train, I carried the taste of her on my tongue, her smell on my fingertips.

Such intangibles—even the autumn light spilling through the salt-sprayed glass is more real. With her resting in the crook of my arm, I told her: "Imagine light scrubbed bare, then gold-leafed."

I said: "The walls of the house are wood."

I said: "When I take you there, the seagulls will wake you every morning."

I leave her with impressions of a house she may never see. And the rest of what I leave is gone before I reach the corner—the teacups washed, the ashtray emptied, Agnes in the shower scrubbing me from her body with a soap that smells of sage.

I look up, and Lisa's staring at me, her eyes so intense, I can't think of anything to do except smile. When she doesn't smile back, I lay down the book of poems, cross the narrow band of floor between us, and kiss her.

We lie together, squeezed onto the narrow sofa. Lisa has one bare leg thrown across my legs. I wonder how many times we've done this, ended an argument with sex. Finally, it's easier. No one has to accept blame or puzzle out what really made us argue. Our bodies forge a resolution for a time. But then time passes, and though the circumstances change, someone is hurt again, someone slams a door again, someone leaves the house again, and we're no closer to understanding why.

In the almost two months I've known Agnes, I can't imagine trying to distract her from what she wants to say. In our conversations, she wants reasons, wants to ferret out my motives, make me admit what's on my mind. "Maybe some things don't need to be talked to death," I've told her. Smiling sometimes, she responds, "Why are you so afraid of what you feel?"

We've had two arguments, and I'm not sure the first (about the best way to prime a particular grade of canvas) qualifies as anything more than a minor disagreement. And the second might not have been an argument either, but her voice tensed when she said, "Believe me, I know you. I pay very close attention."

Because I had said, "You don't even know me. We've seen each other, what? A half dozen times?"

"Seven," she said.

Lisa slides her hands beneath my shirt and strokes my back, and after a moment she leans away enough to look up at me.

She says, "What were you thinking?"

"When?" I murmur.

She tilts her head to indicate the other couch. "Over there," she says. "Before you kissed me."

"Mm." I pull her back to me and kiss her forehead. "I don't remember," I say. "Let's take a nap."

"Christ," she says as she struggles away from me and sits up on the sofa. When I ask what's wrong, she says, "I have work to do," and reaches down to the floor to separate her jeans and underwear from the tangle of clothes. Scowling, she stands, looking down at me as she steps into her pants and tugs the zipper up on her jeans. She picks up her socks and shoes and sits on the other sofa to put them on.

Watching her, I wonder when I came to feel so distant. I've left her as surely as if I'd walked out of the room. What remains is emptiness that I both cause and occupy. I don't want her to be unhappy. If I can avoid hurting her, I will. But as she sits on the sofa lacing up her shoes, I know that what I feel for her is simply the affection I'd feel for any other friend. Strangely, this realization feels like my true betrayal. Falling out of love is not what I expected.

"What's this you're reading?" Lisa says, looking down at the book on the cushion beside her.

I tell her the title, though she's reading it from the cover. "Where'd you pick this up?" she says, beginning to page through it. For a moment I can't remember if Agnes's name is on the flyleaf, if she's made notes in the margins, marked favorite lines. But there's no edge to Lisa's question; I tell her the name of a used bookstore not far from our apartment in Center City.

She says, "Since when do you read poetry?"

I repeat what Agnes said: "All painters should know Rilke."

She flips through the book, pausing to read a line here and there, before closing it gently and laying it on the coffee table. She studies it for a few seconds before looking up at me. "If you haven't already read Rilke, how do you know that?" she asks.

I make myself meet her eyes, but I can't make myself speak. *Who is alone now, will remain alone.* After a pause, she gets up, goes to the hall, and puts on her jacket.

As she walks back through the living room, I say, "Going out?"

She opens the French doors and a cold wind pushes past her. "Obviously," she says.

"I thought you had work to do," I say, but she's already closed the doors behind her.

For a while, I lie on the sofa, looking at the map my aunt painted in watercolor, framed, and hung over the mantel when she and Caroline built the cottage in the forties. The paper's water-stained from storms when the chimney flashing didn't hold—a situation I've come to know well since the roof became my responsibility.

Aunt Lou was an Atlanta architect, and the map is labeled in an architect's blocky hand: *Edingsville Beach* and *Frampton Inlet* and *Botany Bay*, and the network of tiny, meandering creeks that reduce the island to little more than chunks of sand surrounded by marsh and water. This house is a mark on the coast, and the Atlantic gradually darkens as it deepens away from shore. Lou drew a cross on the map to show where, on the road leading off the island, an historical marker delineates the high water of the worst coastal flooding on record, in the hurricane of 1899.

When I was a boy, I'd lie on the couch and study the map and think about the ocean covering up all the land where the house is, and the street behind us, the cement-block grocery store and the second-row houses and even the third, all the way past what's now called Jungle Road because it looks more like something you might find deep in the lush interior, not a place where waves ever lapped the low-hanging branches of the palms. At night I had to sleep with the light on. I had nightmares of the waves slamming into the windows, the house filling with salt water.

"Of course it could happen again," Caroline had told me, ignoring my mother's frown. Practical and plainspoken, my aunt's lover taught biology at Agnes Scott and didn't believe in soft-pedaling nature. When we walked the beach together, she'd take a stick to the body of a sea turtle ravaged by gulls, to show me its anatomy. Even at five or six years old, I delighted in this, knowing my mother would've tried to distract me from the carrion by pointing out the light on the water or an interesting formation of clouds.

At night, in the absence of television, Caroline told stories about the early indigo farmers who settled the island, and the cotton plantations that sprang up in the eighteenth century. Descendants of these planters still live on the island, and I was amused that the bedwetting, booger-eating Middleton boy I played with was the remnant of an aristocracy. My favorites among Caroline's stories were the tragedies: the planter's daughter drowned in a storm, the bride murdered on her wedding day by a spurned suitor.

Caroline said with an authority not even my mother questioned that a ghost wearing a blood-stained wedding gown haunted the ruins of Brick House—ruins Caroline and I had explored together on sullen, mosquito-slapping afternoons when Aunt Lou and my mother sat on the porch drinking lemonade and trying to unravel their family's complicated genealogy.

"Who cares who married whom?" Caroline tossed out conspiratorially as I followed her to her car. "What I'm interested in is living history."

When I dared to point out that the ghost wasn't, technically, living history, she looked at me as if I were nuts.

"Of course she is," Caroline said. "She's still there, isn't she?"

Later, when I tried out this reasoning, my mother said, "Caroline has always thought a little differently from most people," and gave me a look that ended the discussion.

The first time I brought Lisa here was on the heels of a February storm. I promised Aunt Lou that "my buddies" and I wouldn't trash the place, and she agreed we could use the house if I promised to repair the porch screens. This was a few years before she died, not long after she'd lost Caroline, and I think now it was the test: Did I love the house enough to make repairs even when I was supposed to be having fun?

Lisa and I had been dating about six months, in the sheltered corral of a college campus. It's easy to forget sometimes how fast things change. Ten years later, it's another world—boys and girls living in the same dormitories, "free love" everywhere you look. Back then we could barely arrange to be alone together. Her parents thought she was spending spring break in Myrtle Beach with her roommates.

It doesn't take much imagination to construct the events of the week we spent here. But we were sloppy enough. By the time we returned to Pennsylvania, she was pregnant, although it took another month before we knew that, and yet another month before we found a doctor who could help us.

Going through that experience was bound to either draw us closer or break us apart completely, and I have to admit that when summer came, I still didn't know which way we'd fallen. I thought Lisa was holding up all right, so I didn't cancel my plans to study in Italy. I'd only been gone a couple of weeks when I got a letter from Lisa's mother, saying that Lisa had been hospitalized for "nervous exhaustion" and not to worry if I didn't hear from her for a while.

Her folks have always been fond of me, and I imagine even if her mother knew about the abortion—which Lisa insists she doesn't—she'd remain fond. I have always been, as Lisa's mother likes to say, "a wonderful young man," by which she means I'm polite, quiet, and generally cheerful, from a good family. She forgives me for being an artist because I talk sports with Lisa's father. She forgives my long hair because when Lisa and I visit, I clean the gutters, fix the leaking faucets, shovel the walks if there's snow. When Lisa and I disagree about something, I can count on her to take my side.

In the autumn when Lisa and I were back in school, I realized that a sticky new web bound us to a path with marriage at its logical end. Lisa reminded me frequently that she'd "been through a lot." And having *been through a lot* apparently entitled her to my life, although I didn't really know why she wanted it. It seemed—still seems—a rough-hewn thing to me.

When I stand up from the couch to get dressed, I see that she hasn't gone far, just down to the ruins of the jetty. I'm putting on my shoes when I see her sit on the sand about ten feet from the edge of the tide. She wraps her arms around her knees and looks out at the ocean, and after a while she leans her forehead against her knees. I'd almost bet she figures I'm watching her, that the wistful pose is for my benefit.

I go into the kitchen to check on dinner. I've lost my appetite. Everything here is more than twenty years out of date—the pots dented, the knives dull—and I know before too long, I'll have to renovate if I want to keep on renting out the place. I can't even imagine the cost of such a project, but I'm certain it's one more thing I don't want to think about.

I take the pan of dressing from the oven, jiggle the bird's leg to be sure it's done. I slice a few tomatoes onto a chipped plate, clean the broccoli—things that, had Lisa really had any interest in making dinner, she could've done once she saw I'd taken care of the main dish.

I take a mug of tea out to the screened porch, thinking I might call Lisa in for dinner, but she's given up sitting on the sand—it must be damp, after all—and is now walking toward the mouth of the river. The shelling beach, Caroline and Lou called it—where the land curves out like a great arm, and sweeps in all the ocean's debris. A twenty-minute walk there, and twenty back—if that's where she's going, by the time Lisa returns, the dressing will be room temperature, the tomatoes leaking juice. I think for a minute about going after her.

Instead, I figure that whatever shape the dinner is in, it'll be more pleasant to eat if she's walked off her mood. I take my tea back into the house, turn off the stove and the kitchen light. In the living room, I stoke the fire, sit on the couch, and open the volume of poems.

The day she gave me the book, Agnes told me that Rilke was married to a sculptor, a woman I'd never heard of. Soon after their child was born, he left them. To my surprise, Agnes didn't say what I was expecting—what Lisa would have said—that the guy was a creep and a coward. She said, "He knew he couldn't live with them and continue to do his work."

"His wife must've hated him," I said, and she shook her head.

"They saw one another from time to time. His wife knew what he needed, probably as much as he did. Certainly she knew her own needs, although as an artist, she never had his genius."

"I can't imagine they really loved each other," I said.

Agnes sipped her tea. After a while, she said, "It's difficult to judge someone else's life."

As we sat there in her kitchen, Agnes's slate-colored eyes kept darting to the clock over the stove. I had a train to catch. The class her husband taught was ending soon. She had plans to attend a friend's opening. She could have been gauging the time for any of these events, or for none of them. Maybe checking the clock was simply a nervous habit. I didn't know her well enough to be sure. We were—are—still new enough together that if I were to catch my train and never come back, I'd be no more than an odd episode that ended as abruptly and mysteriously as it began.

And while walking out of Agnes's life that way already seems impossible, I never thought I'd have an affair until the night someone who knows us both said, "Henry, here's someone you've got to meet."

I thought I knew myself pretty well. I trusted what I was capable of. As I sat at Agnes's kitchen table holding the volume of Rilke, she turned to me and said, "I love you," and I said, "You hardly know me," and she said, "Believe me, I know you."

On the front porch, Lisa's stomping the sand off her shoes, and in a moment she's in through the French doors and standing before the fire again, removing her jacket, shaking her long blonde hair out around her shoulders.

"Dinner smells fantastic," she says, smiling.

My mother often tells me what a good sport my wife is, and at moments like this, I understand what she means. I can tell by Lisa's voice that she's forgiven me, that somewhere between the jetty and the shelling beach, her anger became so much spindrift. I can almost guess that as she walked into the wind, she told herself, *Don't ruin the holiday. It's just a goddamned chicken. You should be grateful he likes to cook.*

I close the book and lay it aside as she walks over to the couch. Her face is pink from the wind, and her blue eyes seem anxious as she looks down at me and extends her hands. I take hold of them—cold and a little damp—and she hoists me to my feet.

"I'm starving," she says.

"Well," I tell her, "you've come to the right place."

Songs Without Words

In the late afternoon when the sky turns gold you leave your husband reading in the house at the edge of the dunes and walk down to the sea, wearing your blue coat, a hat pulled over your hair. The two dogs trot ahead of you, straining against their leashes. The tide's out. You lunge along the lip of the ocean. Its voice changes according to what it throws itself against, a sound like hot fat in a pan or gravel poured through a paper cylinder. You've stood on both sides of the Atlantic, looked down at it from mountains and across it from low, sandy beaches. You've seen it gray, green, silver, even black in moonlight, but hardly ever blue.

On this southern coast, the beach is a swath of sand, and a long path up through sea oats. A hundred yards inland clapboard houses weather the sea wind, lights already yellowing their windows.

The dogs trot in unison, pulling so hard they cough, a terrible, choking sound as if they've swallowed bones. They're intent on puzzling out a smell. There was no pain killer prescribed after you had the bitch spayed. She lay in her bed and groaned, looking up at you with a haggard, puzzled face, trusting that you had nothing to do with her misery.

A high, thin wind whistles in your ears. Your blood pumps. The dogs pant. As you stand watching the ocean throw itself against the shore, you feel something shift inside you. A barrier moves into place between you and the rest of the world.

Back home in Philadelphia, you sit in the car at a stoplight, weeping. You tell yourself not to be absurd, that surely something was wrong, some genetic foul-up, some physical deformity that made your body decide to shut gestation down. You think of the on-call doctor at the clinic, someone you'd never met, telling you slowly, deliberately, as if you were simple or daft, that nothing you'd done or thought could have caused you to lose the baby.

You stared back at him, having never imagined until that moment that anyone else might suspect that something you'd done was the reason your body rejected this child. He showed you charts, the percentages and figures, tried to reassure you that loss was nothing special. Your pain was ordinary pain. This happens all the time. You'd be surprised how often, he said. And an afterthought: At least you know you can get pregnant, as if you'd had great luck in a trial run.

But this was not supposed to be the trial run; you did that years ago. You wonder if there is a god after all, and if that god is a vengeful god: an eye for an eye, a child for a child.

You shouldn't even be thinking about that child as you stare through the windshield at the line of preschoolers on a field trip, trudging along the sidewalk, their mittened hands clutching at a rope, a teacher at each end. Wearing bright jackets against the spring chill, the children move unsteadily over the brick walk, learning by touch as their free hands trail across the windows and stones of the buildings they pass.

They're younger than your first child would be, if you'd allowed her (you are certain it was a girl) to live. For years, you've thought of that child as *the baby*. That baby is perpetually infant, now with an infant sibling, the one you wanted to be born. A voice in your head sneers, *Now that it's convenient.* You want to ask somebody, *When is it ever convenient? Who gets to choose?*

You chose. There is no cause and effect. The first child did not take away the second. It feels no malice toward you because it was not a being. You know this rationally. In fact, you have sometimes gone weeks without thinking about the baby. Until lately.

As they amble down the sidewalk, you search the children's faces for familiar details: your eyes, his mouth, the cornsilk hair you both had as children. When the car behind you sounds its horn you realize the children have passed.

The word *nurture* as applied to plants is now rife with ambiguity. Every spring for years you have made a garden, even though you only rent the ground you live on. From catalogs you chose packets of seeds and bought plants from the greenhouse. You called the result *profusion*. Yes, you grow a profusion of flowers. They all have names: *angelica* and *iris, black-eyed susan, marguerite, sweet william, daisy, veronica, rose*. You know each one's habits and requirements, common pests, ideal exposure. You know the signs of sickness and disease. Now, this concentration on botanical life seems the worst kind of transference, a total sham.

This spring you look from your upstairs window at the irregular beds where the plants sleep. The dried stems of last year's flowers show where each is buried. You should have clipped them, raked the debris, mulched against the frost. Your neglect is visible to anyone who passes. You do not deserve to call yourself a gardener.

You're almost certain that someone else planted these beds. She worked the earth with your hands, spotted weeds with your blue eyes, but she was not you. All morning you haven't stirred beyond this room. You couldn't make a cup of tea, much less plan something so intricate as a garden. Brown and brittle from the snow-bite, the roses by the front steps clutch the hem of your skirt when you go out or in.

Thank god, it wasn't an actual person. I mean, it's not like you lost a real baby.

Did they tell you what was wrong with it?

I know someone who lost three before she carried to term.

When you think of all the women who get pregnant and don't want kids, it just doesn't seem fair.

For a child to die before the parent is just unnatural.

Believe me, Lisa, it could be so much worse.

So much worse. You picture a heaven populated entirely by children, floating in static like that of the TV screen when the stations go off the air. Your children are there, each one as long as a cocktail shrimp.

Perhaps the story is that all these years you've misunderstood. The marvel is not that children die but that so many survive.

You're a woman who thinks things through, who holds her heart in check until she's sure it won't be broken. But tonight you're one person in a crowd sipping wine in a friend's kitchen, almost certain that you are, quite unreasonably, selfishly, heartbroken, your loss a drop in an endless sea of losses.

Get over it, you tell yourself, smiling fiercely at your friends. Get over it right now.

When you leave them, escape to the deck for air, your friends' voices float through the open doors. *We lost our first child twenty years ago,* a man says, *and I don't think Betsy ever got over it.*

They tell each other you're taking it well, that you're a trooper, that *Lisa is tough as nails, an absolute rock.* They're talking about someone else, they'd have to be . . . you lift another glass of wine to your lips.

Out here it's just you and the cool spring night, the moon rising through the pine boughs, and a form disappearing through the back gate into the alley—just a shape scissoring across the darkness, too distant to identify. The gate clicks shut, and you know that you haven't imagined it entirely. Something was there, yes, circumscribed by absence.

All week you're sure you've misplaced something though you can't imagine what. You open your wallet and count your credit cards. You spill the contents of your jewelry box onto the bed and put the pieces back, one by one. In the warm light of early evening you stand in the yard and look up at your house, your eyes moving from window to window, trying to remember. *Was there somewhere to go? Someone to call?*

In the shower after a long day working in the yard together, your husband soaps your back. The radio is tuned to jazz, Chet Baker's slow voice wrapped around "It's Always You." Henry sings along, working the soap across your shoulders, down the length of your spine, making the clean, bitter smell of lavender rise from your body.

You close your eyes and concentrate on the music as he reaches around and soaps your breasts, so small and ineffectual. He still loves your body, though month after month, it betrays you.

As you lift your face into the spray you know you will lie down together, as if in a dance you've learned. He puts his hand here, you touch him there, your mouths join, you move to a rhythm already playing in your head.

Afterward, you consult the calendar. *Do you know what today is?* you ask, hoping even into his silence that he will know immediately that this was the day set aside for the birth, the date you might have entered into the record books, written on documents, celebrated.

How many years before this date passes unremarked? Each time it will catch you unaware, standing in line in the grocery store, writing a check or a letter, glancing at the newspaper.

Due date, as if for a bill that has to be paid.

Another date when nothing took place.

Behind the beach house you see something glimmer through the trees. Shard of glass. Shimmer of light. Serrated edge of an idea you have learned to live with: You continue to exist. The sun goes down on the other side of the island. On this side, the light just gradually seeps away.

You've unleashed the dogs, and now they snuffle in the underbrush around the cottage. A jay flits from tree to tree, its cries like bits of argument sifting down to where you stand on the wooden walk.

This solitude: how a child would alter it, chattering, dawdling to pick up shells, tripping over the spaces between the boards.

Trying to imagine how the ocean might look to a child seeing it for the first time, you turn and squint out at the water, hands jammed in your front pockets, resting on the hard, narrow crests of your hipbones.

Everything is yet to be named. The ocean turns from gray to black to luminous. You try to think of all the words you need to make sense of what you see around you, but nothing comes. Instead you close your eyes and listen to the ocean or the wind in the scrubby trees, whatever makes up the great silence behind the small silences you accumulate.

Schubert's songs flood the fire-lit room, an arrangement of lieder, a cycle in which words have been simplified to elemental feeling. The dogs sleep, pink bellies turned to the heat, feet jerking as they dream. Two of them: You wonder if your entire life is nothing but compensation. Sitting beside your husband, you sip tea and watch the oak logs blaze.

A storm tonight, the shift in season, rain ticking at the windows as the dialogue between cello and piano ebbs and surges.

Under the blanket of sounds, if you could speak of how you feel, what would you say? Deep inside your chest, a vibration thrums against the hollows. The dogs raise their heads and stare at you, bewildered, waiting for your voice. You imagine your words would be so accurate and interior, they'd brush the inside of your eyelids, sift into your throat, fill the space around what's said to be your heart. You imagine they might even touch the man whose child you want to bear.

You set the teacup carefully on the table as your husband reaches for you. How much of this is habit, how much desire, how much the need for simple touch, you can't begin to say. The ocean roars and rain chatters at the windows, complicated measures scored to fit your life. They're nothing you've said, played back to you in rhyme. They're the silence you open yourself into, the duet between time and your body.

What Is

Henry broke his dying to me gently. Last summer, on our first trip alone together since Emma's birth, he pulled me down beside him on a narrow strip of sand, our derelict cottage twenty yards away. He took the camera from my hands, held my fingers tight between his own, and said, "This time next year, I'll be somewhere out beyond the breakers."

It was barely morning, the sun a pink smear over water. The tide was coming in. I fingered the cuff of his blue shirt and tried to stop what I was feeling. We sat looking at the water, watching the pelicans dive.

In the photograph I took before he relieved me of the camera, Henry's in a blue shirt and jeans, blue eyes fixed on something off the picture plane. His long white hair disappears behind his shoulders and he leans back upon his hands.

The night before, tired after the long drive down but happy to be back in Carolina, we'd made love, and as he worked his fingers through the tangles in my hair, I'd said I hoped we'd conceived a second child.

Henry had a particular way of seeing, a way of showing how the abstract concept gives way to the tangible image. As he spoke to me on the beach that morning, I watched seagulls squabble and scavenge, and I tried not to think of how our life together would cease to be. This is where he wanted his ashes scattered, the beach he'd loved since childhood, where he brought Lisa and their son years before Emma and I came along. Maybe the mutations in the cells began when he was just a kid sitting cross-legged on the sand, the sun beating down on his blond head bent over a sand castle.

I sat beside him, leg against his leg, our hands entwined as if that would keep the world from sliding out from under us. I thought of all I needed to remember of this moment—his touch, for instance, and the way he could occupy the space and still leave room for me. He smoked a cigarette while my list grew longer, encompassing smell and taste and texture, the pulse of waves breaking, my impulse to cling to him as Emma had when we dropped her off at my sister's, weeping bitterly and pleading not to be left behind.

After a while he said, "Emma will need boots and a new coat before the snow comes." He was cataloging, too, making lists of what he might accomplish before the cancer did its work, before the fire took away his body, before waves closed over the shards of bone and gravity pulled them to the depths.

Our stone house in Pennsylvania lies far from any shore—no bay or ocean, no lake or river, not even a creek or stream complicates the geography of this university town, where the industry's intellectual, requiring no water to turn its wheels. Henry's grandfather built our house in 1929, and only Henry's family has ever owned it. Henry's grandfather was a professor of agronomy, Henry's father an army officer. After a childhood on the move, I think Henry liked the idea of having this solid old place to come back to.

What we lack in water, we make up in stone. An obelisk on campus shows the geological formation of the earth on which it stands, rock striated by age: granite, limestone, slate, shale. Leaving the daycare this afternoon, I push Emma past it in her stroller and wonder if the stone continues to change even when it's brought above the surface. Perhaps Emma's thrice-great grandchildren will see the shale becoming slate, notice the formation of the first fragile layer of permeable stone in what looks to me like a scrim of fine dust.

Even as an adult, Henry lived other places, teaching here and there until the illustration jobs became more regular. At forty, when his mother died, he brought his family here, turned an enclosed porch into a studio, and started writing and illustrating children's books. The year we met, he was a finalist for the Caldecott Medal, though he thought the nominated book was far from being his best.

I loved them all, can still lose myself in the worlds he created, just as I did as a child. With a little more time, he could have finished Emma's book, a story she heard but won't remember.

As I push Emma's stroller across the campus quad, I can't help thinking that time is what we never had enough of, even after Emma was born and we both worked at home. Through the French doors, I'd glimpse him hunched over his drafting table, white hair a line down the center of his back, a cigarette burning in the ashtray. In our three-year marriage, we spent most of every day together, but now it seems I hardly saw him. I try to fix in memory what there was to Henry, who was always not just any man. He's two months dead, and I tell myself his hair was white as moonlight on the coldest winter night. My next thought is, his hair still had a tinge of blond.

Emma's blond hair will darken as she ages. She has my brown eyes. "Co, co, co," she urges, pushing against the front bar of her stroller. If I ran, she'd want me to run faster. She loves to travel, to go, to be in transition from the familiar to the unknown. When she recognizes our street, she whines to keep me walking, knowing a nap waits in ambush, hidden among her playthings or in some corner of a room. My breath is a thin white mist jetting from my mouth, and when she looks up to urge me on, Emma's breath is just the same.

The night she was born, Henry helped me breathe her into being. He held my shoulders, telling me when to push or rest, and stepping in so Emma slid into his hands. His was the first face she gazed into, the one she'll spend her lifetime trying to recall.

"Co, co, co, co, co," she cries out as we race along the sidewalk, her syllables round and clear as crystal beads flung across a tabletop.

Since Henry's death, I've gone back to Accu-Weather, resuming my life as part-time doyenne of computer-generated design. Emma and I are home by three-fifteen, like latchkey kids with no parent underfoot. I give her a plastic pan of crayons and three feet of brown kraft paper. She stretches out on top of it, coloring from top to bottom, hand moving in an arc.

If Emma were a color, it would be carmine. Her fat feet in fuzzy socks, round diapered bottom in snap-legged cords, warm shirt in cotton knit—all red, just like the color she grinds into the paper on top of orange and yellow, recording something of her day. She murmurs to the paper beneath her hand, then looks up at me, eyes shining like beach glass.

"What?" I say, and smile at the sly look that overtakes her face. She holds out three fingers.

"I free," she says.

"You little fox," I say. "You're not three. You're two years old."

"No," she says, shaking her head, for a moment looking just like Henry in her stubbornness. She goes back to coloring her page, clearly put out with me for disagreeing.

Henry would agree that she was queen if that's what she told him, her face growing more and more astonished at what she could get him to believe.

For which of us will Henry's death be the greater tragedy? My family and friends act as if losing Henry is an abrasion that will eventually scab over. My friend Marie—thirty, and on her second marriage—took me out for coffee yesterday and said, *You don't want to think about this now, sweetie, but you know you'll find someone else. You're twenty-five, for god's sake, you'll turn to stone if you don't love again, you'll become a keeper of cats, old before your time.* Trying to make me laugh, she tousled my hair and said, *No sex for the next sixty years? Impossible, Kerry!* My aunt Liz, who lost her first husband in the Iraq war, phoned last week to talk about how life goes on. And as she talked, I saw how the story's supposed to go: The memory of Henry grows bleary, the early marriage gets mentioned in a footnote, becomes a brief episode and not the central story. Anything else means I'm a bit deranged.

Emma has Henry indelibly at her core. Already I see evidence of his supple mind and stubborn streak and a kinder heart than mine. I think the part that Henry hated most about dying was that this child he loved more than life itself wouldn't remember that she napped beside him on the sofa, or that sometimes he danced her to sleep, or that when they sailed boats in her bath and he boomed "Anchors Aweigh," she shrieked and pounded the water in delight, a little Neptune churning the waves.

Twenty hours a week I make the weather. I turn text into illustration, as if words alone can't convey what the forecasters mean. This morning I made storm clouds roll across my computer screen, pushing today's weather out to sea. Snow blanketed the northern tier, but fell scattered below I-80. On the website, these February days show up purple, blue, or white. Clouds and snowflakes are all we need on the border legends. I pointed and clicked and saved the day, banked it as weather yet to come.

What I see from Henry's studio window looks nothing like the day I made up yesterday. The sky, thick as batting, turns a color I couldn't replicate if I tried, silvery-blue tinged with purple at the edges, while at the center it's white-washed almost tame. While Emma colors fire onto her paper, I watch the sky through a screen of trees.

A chance of snow, a frozen stillness, a February afternoon. A good day to stay indoors, with a good book and a shot of something warm. From where I stand, all that moves are a few birds flying in the distance. Even the trees look frozen, and the clouds look chilled to a solid mass. I don't mind the weather being cold, especially if I'm inside.

Henry used to walk in every kind of weather, come home soaked or sunburned or so cold, his hands felt like slabs of ice on my breasts and I would pull away, laughing. The weather of his books, conveyed in paint and paper, is real down to the strength of light and the way the shadows fall. He could replicate at midnight the light we'd seen at noon, bring home the color of the ocean, render the black inside of a tulip with such exactitude I'd forget that tulips were weeks from blooming, that the garden lay deep under snow.

I asked: *How do you remember?*

He said: *How could I forget?*

On the floor, Emma's grown quiet, and when I look, she's fallen asleep on top of her drawing, cheek pressed to a crimson flame. Only in sleep is she ever silent.

I carry her to the couch and while I'm covering her with a blanket, the mail drops through the slot in the front door. Still the condolences come from people far away, the slow trickle of word-of-mouth, what someone said to someone who's in touch with someone else: *Henry was a lovely man and it's really such a shame.* Today there's a plain vellum envelope with something thick inside, addressed in a spidery blue scrawl, and Lisa's name above a return address in California.

We met for the first and only time at Henry's funeral. Lisa sat in the last row alone, and when I looked back she gazed at me with a calm and contemplative expression. I felt shabby and disarranged, with cat hair on my sweater and a snag in my black tights. I hadn't slept much the last week of Henry's life or in the days since his passing.

After the service, when Lisa took me carefully into her arms, I felt like collapsing against her shoulder. In her smart black suit, silk blouse, and black heels, her silver hair in a sophisticated bob, she looked every inch the widow, though her eyes were dry and clear. Lisa loved him many years more than I did, bore him a son before I was born, and when they parted after twenty years of marriage, she moved across the country. So far as I know, she hadn't seen or spoken to Henry in years.

In the church vestibule, she did not tell me she'd always gone on loving him. She did not say she regretted the years they spent apart. She said gently, "My heart breaks for you and Emma," but I saw her heart had broken, healed, and was broken again by Henry's passing. As I stood beside her, I thought, I know nothing about love.

I tear open the envelope and inside, there's an ivory card with Lisa's initials monogrammed on the front in silver. Inside the card she's tucked two black-and-white photographs of Henry she found after his funeral. She speaks again of her sympathy for me, says she believes I might want the photographs for Emma, whom she calls *Henry's beautiful little girl*. She closes with the word, *Warmly*, and she's right, the note is warm but careful not to overstep whatever bounds exist between us.

I take the photographs to the window and look at each one closely. In the first, Henry is six or seven, standing on a dusty patch of ground in what looks like New Mexico or Arizona, some dry place with a forsaken, cast-off look that marks it as the 1940s. He's grinning at the camera, squinting in the midday sun. His hair's so blond, even then it seems white. He wears a short-sleeved shirt, dark shorts, and sandals, and his right arm is in a cast.

In the other photo, he looks about twenty, surrounded by a group of laughing people in a bar with a tropical theme. All their faces shine with sweat, and everyone looks a little drunk. In a white, open-collared shirt, Henry's sandwiched between two dark girls, and snakes an arm around each one's waist. I turn it over: in Henry's hand, the inscription *Panama, 1957.*

I make myself another cup of tea and sit at the window beside Henry's work table, looking out at a sky turned gray and rose and luminous as quartz, as if air could turn to hard, thin stone. Henry never told me he'd been to Panama, never mentioned a broken arm, and yet these are things Lisa must've known so well she didn't think they'd need an explanation.

I think of the nights Henry and I lay together, telling stories of our pasts, the places we'd been and the people we'd let down or who'd let us down, and the people we hoped we wouldn't fail. Married to Lisa, Henry had a wrenching love affair that caused a kind of veil to drop over his eyes the single time he mentioned it, and he provided few details. All I could offer in return were stories of fumbling adolescent passions, this boy, that guy, someone who'd wanted to hook up or get laid.

Henry told me about living in Mississippi in the early 1950s, about spending his later teens in France. Sometimes he'd say things, like *My god, Kerry, my mother would've loved you!* or *You should have seen Berlin that soon after the war*, that made me feel I'd come along too late, would never catch up with all he'd seen, all he knew.

When he told me about clipping playing cards onto the spokes of his grandmother's bicycle, he had to explain gas rationing. He was forty-five when he bought his first computer; I started kindergarten that year, and learned to use one, too.

I'll be the one to bring Henry back to life for Emma, who otherwise will know him only as a name and a face from photographs transposed dimly into memory. Now I know he broke his arm, he went to Panama. But Emma will want to know, How did he break his arm? Why was he in Panama? I can't help but leave out some critical details. Who taught him to cut her pancakes into a sunflower shape? I never thought to ask. I never asked him when he saw the ocean for the first time, or what he thought about on his long walks, or why the blue mug was his favorite. I don't remember where he started school, or the name of the town where he lived in Mississippi. Did I ever know the name of his best friend when he lived in Germany, the name of the girl he took to his senior prom? If I did, it's lost.

The sky's overlaid with black branches, and the street winds into a black line up the snow-covered hill. Crows mass in the elms, a last gathering before nightfall. They rise and settle, rise and lift their wings, one occasionally flying off and then circling back to claim its place among its kin. Crows were Henry's favorite bird, and he often drew them. He sat here often, just staring out, learning what bound them up with humans.

One afternoon last autumn, before Henry got too sick, we took a drive in the country. As we came up over a ridge, we saw two crows in the opposite lane. One looked dead, but the other was just standing beside it on the blacktop, like a seagull sunning itself on the beach.

"Dumb bird," I said. "Somebody's going to run over it."

Henry stopped the car on the shoulder, got out, and walked back to the two birds. The sentry crow fluttered up, making a racket as it swept around overhead. I looked away as Henry picked up a rock and brought it down hard on the other bird's skull. When Henry walked back to the car, the sentry crow landed beside its companion, made a few jabs at the dead bird with its beak, then flew off.

"Poor bird was still alive," Henry told me as he started the car.

"How did you know?" I asked.

He shrugged. "No crow ever dies alone," he said.

After Emma's been fed and bathed, she lies in a bed built low so she won't get hurt if she tumbles out. She curls at the center surrounded by her stuffed animals and picture books, legs drawn up under a quilt made from fabric the color of bittersweet, sunlight, the deep brown humus of the forest floor, the red of a cardinal's wing, hues of goldenrod and amber, as if color alone could keep her warm.

"Papa home?" she asks drowsily while I sit stroking her hair, waiting for sleep to come and take her.

I tuck her hair behind her ear and kiss her. She doesn't press for an answer, but every night she asks the question.

It must seem to her that Henry's gone out on one of his long walks. He liked the ploughed fields beyond the edges of development, the hemmed-in meadows that still ring our growing town. He walked for miles, but by this winter's solstice, he couldn't walk across the room.

When Emma falls into a drowse, I sit on the wide sill of her bedroom window and wait for her breath to become heavy and regular. Her windows look out on our small back yard, covered in snow for weeks. And now more snow is falling. A dry snow, I can tell by the way it drifts; come tomorrow, I'll be able to sweep it from the sidewalk like sand. It mounds in the concrete birdbath, delineates the crossbeams on the arbor. I look down onto the ornamental trees near the house and see each branch as two lines, white over black, stark and simple. The collage of gray near the alley is a deciduous hedge backed by the almost-black of the yew. The gray sky cups over us, shaking out snow like bits of spume.

The first time I came to this house, it was early summer. The windows were open to the dark back yard. Something sweet from outside scented the rooms, and Henry told me the sweet olive tree was in bloom. He'd invited me over to see the illustrations for the book he was just finishing.

We'd met at a party the evening before, when he asked me if I liked a particularly obnoxious painting on our host's living-room wall. Without the confidence to say no, I tried to turn the question back to him. He wouldn't let me, pressing me until I admitted I thought the painting "lame."

"Define 'lame,'" he insisted, and supplied question after question until I described the harshness of color, the aggression of the line, the "self-indulgent anger" that pervaded the whole work. At that point Henry broke into a grin and said, "It's an early work of mine."

When I went to Henry's house—this house, my house now—I wanted to see his work. I also wondered what I'd do if he came on to me. He was older than my father, and yet the way he talked to me didn't seem paternal. We had tea, we looked at the illustrations, we walked around the garden just as dusk was falling, and he told me the house's history. He told me things about the town I didn't know, though I'd lived here all my life.

I drank so much tea I got jittery from the caffeine and asked question after question, until I think Henry must have suspected I just didn't want to leave. That's when he walked me to my car. I made up an excuse to see him again, and then another. When I was on the verge of making a fool of myself, he finally invited me to dinner.

As he opened the wine that night, he said wryly, "I wasn't sure if I was imagining things. I thought, You old coot, don't flatter yourself."

From then on, my life seemed composed of intervals between times of seeing Henry. He talked to me like no one ever had, and I couldn't get enough of what he had to tell me. He knew things about animals, about the planets and stars, about people I'd never heard of. He showed me how to identify trees, and where the rabbits had their burrow, and when the moon waxed or waned. When we took walks, he pointed out different styles of architecture where I had just been seeing houses. We'd sit out on the porch in good weather, late into the night, smoking cigarettes and talking, talking, talking.

When cold weather came, we moved indoors, to the living room in front of the open fire. What blared from his CD player was Mozart and Telleman and Haydn, occasional Vivaldi, copious Grieg and Sibelius. These were composers I'd barely heard of, having spent my life with headphones jacked in to Tori Amos and Ani DeFranco.

He said I was an emissary from another world, that he loved my endless questions and curiosity, my enthusiasm about things he'd long since stopped noticing or wondering about. He said he loved the way I could spend hours piecing together a quilt, the way I could untangle the worst problems on his computer, the way I smelled just stepping out of the bath.

But even as we fell in love, Henry had a tremendous reluctance to involve me in his life. He was tender, always kind, although a few times he lost patience with my refusal to understand what I was—as he liked to say—letting myself in for.

I said I could take care of myself. He said I had no idea what kind of strings love was capable of weaving. I accused him of being afraid to love me. He accused me of being too selfish to love anyone but myself. Then he apologized, and admitted he was afraid.

He said, "I'm almost forty years older than you are. If you were in my place, you'd be terrified."

I said, "Nothing's guaranteed. I could get killed by a car tomorrow. Then what?"

When I got pregnant, we had our fiercest argument. He kept saying, "Having a baby is not like taking in a stray cat, Kerry. You have no idea how our life is about to change."

And Henry was right: Our life changed with Emma's birth, and mine will go on changing. But had she not been born, my life would have also altered. Meeting him changed me. Every time we talked, I felt the world crack open a little wider.

I see now that Henry wanted me to learn all I could about the world without ever being bruised by it. The night before he died, I sat beside him on the bed we'd brought into his studio. The hospice nurse had come and gone, and it was black outside the windows. We sat watching the candle flames flicker bright against the cold glass. Blowing through the trees, the wind sounded like waves breaking.

I asked: *If you had it to do over, would you unravel it?*

He turned his head on the pillow and looked at me for a long while. He said: *You know I wouldn't.*

The small hours are the longest, when the boiler in the basement comes to life with a jolt, and I wake from a restless sleep. I keep my eyes closed, hoping to avoid what I've come to know too well, the insomnia that persists until morning. Steam rises in the radiators, a process I track mentally until the route becomes too diffuse to follow. Beams in the attic creak, and the house seems to stretch out in sleep, flexing its limbs. Wind fills the huge fir trees at the end of the yard and the sound is like waves washing in, then washing out again.

I turn over in bed and open my eyes. The snow has stopped. Through the lace curtain, the full moon shines in a clear black sky, and its light falls over the foot of the bed. I sit up. The light seems a passage into another world, a window to slip through.

In Henry's books, children were always discovering unlikely routes to the unexpected: *What is never seems,* he liked to say, *and what seems hardly ever is.*

What world would this light be, if he were here to make it? Before I have thought much past *illuminated, complicated,* Emma appears at my bedroom door, in her red fleece sleeper.

She says the moon woke her.

"It woke me up, too," I tell her.

So we're awake here together in the hard hours, in a room filled with moonlight and a sound like the ocean. She stands in the doorway, barefoot, rubbing the side of her head. Nothing seems more natural than to throw back the blanket, expose the cold side of the bed and tell her to snuggle in beside me.

But I find my slippers in the dark and go to her. When I pick her up, she locks her arms around my neck and whispers, "Turn it down, Mama."

"The moon?" I ask, and she nods against my neck.

I almost tell her that I'm not the parent who had that power, the gift of taking reality and shaping it into something extraordinary, but what good would that do at this time of night?

"I'll give it a try," I say, carrying her back into her own moonlit room.

After

When the telephone rang this evening, I let the machine pick up as usual, but after the first few words I was across the room with the receiver in my hand. *Miss Landowska, you don't know me. My name is Ben Tillman and my father was a friend . . .*

The voice sounded so like his father's, Henry himself might have been at the other end of the line. But Henry never telephoned. *A clean break* is the cliché he used—he wanted nothing that would ache on days when there was a promise of rain.

For thirty-five years, Henry's had his own room in my imagination, a quiet place where the lights have gradually grown dim. All that time, he's been standing at the black window, watching harbor lights twinkle faintly in the distance, listening to the sea wind blow. But now he turns from the window and walks to the battered armchair covered in fabric so worn the pattern's indistinct. He sits down, turns on the lopsided floor lamp, picks up his glass of wine and a dog-eared copy of *Art in America*, the issue with my painting on the cover. He turns the pages slowly. Eventually, he comes to the feature story. He looks at my photograph and thinks (for this is my fantasy, I can have him think what I wish), *Leaving her was the biggest mistake I ever made.* The windows rattle, the ocean slaps the sand, a fire springs to life in the hearth. I make him sit like that for hours, not out of malice, but because he's holding me in his hands.

He's tired after a full day in the studio, and now it's nearly midnight. His wrists are narrow, tanned, and his hands chapped from the cold. Although I've continued to age, he's just as he was when I last saw him—thirty, blond, a fine-boned, unlined face, and deceptive eyes, a startling dark blue. His eyes are still what I notice first—slightly unequal in size: The right eye opens wider, with a kind expression.

The left one's shrewd and knowing. That's the one I should have paid better attention to.

When the wine is gone, he reaches up and turns off the lamp. For a few minutes, he sits in the dark, fingers laced behind his head, listening to the wind try the windows and whistle through the French doors. Though snow's unlikely on the Carolina coast, he finds himself wishing for it anyway, remembering the winter we knew each other, all those walks in the snow. When he stands and walks into the dark bedroom, I follow. He unbuttons his threadbare shirt, his face a study in concentration, his thoughts absorbed in something other than the task. I stand so close, his faint, peculiar scent comes to me—slightly vegetable in nature, a bit like celery. I recognize it at once, just as I do his body—the fleece across his chest, the muscles of his thighs, the shape of his sex. An ordinary human body, imperfect and beloved. He pulls back the cotton bedspread on the narrow bed. He lies down and closes his eyes.

And suddenly I know the price of my being here: I am not allowed to speak, not allowed to touch him. I sit beside him on the bed and look down into his face. Half my life ago, I'd have given anything to rest my lips against the hollow of his clavicle. Now I look at him with only mild surprise that he's as lovely as I remembered.

He falls asleep, and as I watch, he wades into a scene of final, perfect peace, where the dark sky snags the ocean in its net of stars, leaving a line of phosphorescence in the sand. Gone. Just like that. Eternally just out of reach.

"Miss Landowska?" his son says. "Are you still there?"

Still there. The cottage in Carolina was the only house he ever mentioned; he described the rooms, the view, the smell so vividly I sometimes still dream of it, though for all I know, it was no more real than I was—a temporary fantasy of another kind of life. He placed the cottage in the dunes a stone's throw from the sea, shingled it in cedar, painted blue trim around the doors and windows.

"The Gullah people say blue keeps away the haints," he explained as we hiked our borrowed upstate woods. Headed back to our friend's cabin that frigid afternoon, the sky like silvered glass, I laughed, and said, "In Poland, farmers paint their cottages blue when their daughters are old enough to marry. I remember from my childhood."

"So," he said and smiled. "The same color both entices and keeps away." Beneath the edge of his navy-blue watch cap, his brows gleamed gold and his eyes wrinkled at the corners. I put my gloved hand against his cheek, thinking, *If you leave me, you'll regret it all your life.*

With an arrogance of which only the young are truly capable, I assumed my love gave me a moral right to Henry. The notion that someone I wanted so fiercely might be destined to spend his life with someone else—it never crossed my mind. The ache in my chest when we were apart had a cure, and the cure was simple. If someone had told me then that the ache would become steady and natural as breathing, that the pain of losing Henry was the needle that stitched my life together, what would I have said? Well, *impossible* is one word that comes to mind.

October 1972: I was at the opening of a photography show in a gallery on 57th Street when my old friend Blake appeared, steering by the elbow a man in jeans and a rumpled jacket, blond hair curling below his collar. "You two have got to meet," Blake trilled.

For all I knew, I could've been standing in the sea and a wave had just broken over my head. I thought, *Oh, sweet Jesus.* Even after so long, I can summon back the way Henry's eyes held mine, how his body angled to close the space between us as he reached out to take my hand. His palm against my fingers felt calloused, a square, thick hand with a light touch. I don't recall what we talked about as we stood drinking wine in a corner of the room, or even whose photographs were on display. All that surfaces is that he mentioned he lived in Philadelphia, was only in town for a few days to meet with publishers interested in his illustration work.

The reception ended, and we stepped outside into a spectacular autumn rain, the kind that makes you almost remember that New York's on the ocean. As we huddled in the doorway, he said, "How about we get some coffee?" I said, "Oh hell, let's keep drinking wine." We started walking to a bar that we vaguely remembered being in the neighborhood, getting soaked before we'd gone more than a block or two. As we approached Columbus Circle, he said he'd like to see my work. I said, "I have a bottle of wine at my studio. We can kill two stones with one bird." As long as I knew him, he teased me about that slip of the tongue.

My studio was just another room in my apartment in the garment district, the room with the best light. Riding the subway downtown in silence, our bodies swaying against each other slightly, I realized my young husband was at a conference, something I'd forgotten. I mean, I literally forgot for a while that I was married. Meeting Henry erased Edward from my mental map. When I looked at Henry's hand grasping the pole just above mine, his wedding ring winked back. Henry looked at me, his face serious, and in that moment I had the visceral realization that my life was about to change.

In the studio I moved the paintings out so Henry could see them, then went to the bedroom and took off my wet clothes. I dressed in a loose sweater and jeans, something deliberately unsexy. I toweled my hair dry and combed it straight behind my ears. I put on my glasses. I told myself that there was nothing wrong with inviting a fellow painter in to look at my new work. All we'd talked about so far was painting and photography. For a moment I even imagined my husband and Henry becoming such good friends that Edward would champion his work, review it enthusiastically as he could not do with mine, get other critics interested. Without ever setting eyes on Henry's paintings, I began to like the idea of being important to his career. Barefoot, I walked into the kitchen, uncorked a bottle of cabernet and brought the bottle and two glasses to the doorway of the studio.

I've learned a lot over the years about people by the way they look at paintings. Henry sat in the old wooden chair I'd pulled out for him, elbows on his knees, pure concentration on his face. He was soaking wet. Occasionally he'd stand and move closer to a painting, crouch to see it better, move it here or there to better catch the light. This went on until I handed him his glass, and he said, "I knew from talking to you that they'd be good, but I had no idea how good."

"And how good are they?"

He went on to tell me. I'd never had anyone look so closely at my work, or talk about it so incisively. He seemed to understand my aims immediately and how I was trying to reach them. He saw where I was struggling. He made links between my work and that of painters I hadn't even thought about, but when he said their names, I saw how a little study might be useful.

He said, "I'm a painter in only the loosest sense of the word. Really, I'm an illustrator. But Agnes, you're going to be a really great painter."

I smiled. I had the good grace to say, *Thank you*, and not what I was probably thinking, which was, *Going to be?* I've never lacked confidence in my paintings, though nearly everything in my studio that night would eventually be destroyed or painted over as I kept pushing myself further, moving deeper into pure abstraction. Some of those paintings I literally cut into pieces and collaged onto other canvases.

When we finally left the studio, he was shivering, so I sent him into the bathroom with a towel and instructions for the dryer. While he took a hot shower and dried his clothes, I sat on the sofa drinking wine, smoking, telling myself that in the three years I'd been married, I'd never been unfaithful to my husband, and there was no need to begin complicating my life now.

When he came into the living room, all washed and dried and rumpled, I looked at him and realized I cared little about complications. I poured us both another glass of wine, and we started talking about the parts of our lives that had less to do with painting. Even then I knew that we were sketching in the rough outlines of what we were getting into. He wanted to hear the story of how I'd left Poland, and I simplified as best I could, although back then leaving Poland was never a simple story.

He told me about the medical-illustration work he did in Philadelphia, where his wife attended graduate school. Somewhere along the line, I must have mentioned that Edward was in California until Monday. But soon those lives seemed so much less interesting than painting, and so we went back to talking about painting. Somewhere in the middle of my telling him what I liked and didn't like about Fairfield Porter's work, Henry leaned across and kissed me. Then he took my hands and kissed inside each palm.

Two days later, he left my apartment for the train back to Philadelphia, and I began to know the numbing sprawl of emptiness, of going through the motions. I welcomed Edward home, painted every day, met friends for dinner, but this life became a sham after I'd been with Henry.

If my first mistake was falling in love with Henry, my second had to be that I believed his marriage was a wrinkle I could work around, a minor inconvenience like my own.

I should say that secrecy was in neither of our natures. While the advice columnists insist *He cheats on her, he'll cheat on you. She strays once, she'll never be faithful,* we both knew this was an anomaly in our lives, one we hardly had a choice in. What was between us felt like destiny, as corny as that sounds. What I didn't realize then? Destiny is simply an excuse invented to explain bad choices and missed opportunities.

That winter, Blake's cabin in the Poconos was the midway point where Henry and I stole days together when circumstances would allow—the imaginary weekend retreat, week-long residency, sometimes even a fictional trip to see Blake, a safely committed gay man who inspired jealousy in neither of our partners and provided us both with an extra key.

Outside those woods, how to stay in touch was a constant worry. Had Edward ever bothered looking at the phone bill, I'd have been hard-pressed to explain sixteen calls to Philadelphia in a single month. Had Henry not kept a studio separate from his home, communication would've been considerably more difficult.

When we were together, Henry and I talked like maniacs, one topic tripping over itself as it raced into another, and another. The desire I felt to know him—really know everything about him—was like nothing I'd felt before or since. Voracious. That's the way I felt about Henry. Also insatiable. One afternoon, he answered the telephone and my first words to him were, "Did you have recurring dreams as a child?" Another time it was, "Who taught you to read?"

I think of Henry one particular November midnight, the first time we met at Blake's. As we shivered in the cabin's doorway, watching snow dust the hemlocks on the hill, I leaned against him, took his cold hands in mine, and held them against my breasts. Our bodies fit together perfectly from the start, two halves of something broken and rejoined, if briefly.

With Henry, the separation between my creative life and the rest of life did not exist. Everywhere I looked, I saw a painting. Every time he touched me, I felt some color stir inside my veins—vermilion, crimson—tasted the possibility of a love that fed the creative beast inside each of us, one that wouldn't crumble under familiarity the way my life with Edward had. I still believe that we had that possibility. I knew him instantly. I saw him clear as light.

And what did I see? A man afraid, like many others—afraid of hurting those he loved, of being hurt, of wanting more than he could afford. A man generous and tender, but when the time came, he was colder than glass and his edges twice as sharp. He kept all the promises I was prepared to break—he did not write, he did not telephone—he unlaced his fingers from mine, he said, *I will not leave her*, because, he said, I was stronger and would ultimately survive. Not for the last time, I saw that strength must be its own reward. A mistake to keep my silence, to let him think I swam perfectly at ease in the empty blue-black sea of my own loneliness.

In a house surrounded by woods, I nurse a bedtime glass of wine as I walk from room to room, no one to bother about except a brindled mutt named Mayo, who snuffles at my footsteps, her wrinkled brow heavy over cataract-clouded eyes. I've lived alone here since my daughter went to college, and I love the solitude a little more each year.

On the table by my favorite chair there's Rika's wedding photograph. A tiny thing, auburn-haired and fair-skinned, she must take after someone on Henry's side. Her dark blue eyes seem more determined than innocent. In her white lace dress, she smiles without a trace of irony, twenty-one and already someone's lovely bride. She was the victor in our argument. She would show me how it was done, how simple to have a happy married life, how easy to be ordinary. Rika had her church wedding, her string of bridesmaids, her handsome groom—a kind and decent man, thank god for that.

I put the photo in a drawer when Rika visits, but I like her look of unguarded trust, an expression that—do I need to say?—has long since stopped appearing on her face. The ordinary life she aspired to turns out to have eluded her altogether. A poet, with an ordinary life?

I might have warned her that she couldn't escape herself, though god knows, she still tries.

That's something Henry realized, that he was stuck with who he was. I tried to make him see he could have so much more, if only he'd push harder, not settle for the status quo. You can't escape yourself, but you can transcend your limitations if you're determined. God knows, I've been doing it now for over sixty years.

By April, Henry's wife's intuition had kicked in: The last time we went to Blake's, Lisa phoned a different time each night, always just after we'd made love. She must've heard in his voice that something wasn't right. He closed the bedroom door behind him, took the phone into the other room, so all I heard was low murmuring—faint music if I'd had more wine and hovered closer to the edge of sleep.

I lay in the wrinkled sheets, instructing myself not to listen, not to think beyond my body in the bed, momentarily cut free of all its moorings. Through the uncurtained window some nights I watched stars glint in the black sky, on others watched spring snow fall. Certain that I was losing him, I felt a bit at sea. Henry came back to bed, cold, and wordlessly we lay close, no lies turning us from one another. What could we have said? We were at the far remove of each other's lives even as we lay skin to skin, pages of a story we already knew the end of. My fingers timed the blood beating in his wrist, each second an increment of years we wouldn't share. In my body, Rika had already taken hold.

Love's trajectory always seems a river, unless it snags early on. I found myself behind the dam of my own inability to move forward. My one shred of real happiness became the sieve I wove my life around. Henry wasn't the last man who ever loved me. He wasn't the handsomest, most intelligent, most talented. But he was the man I loved.

Six months we stole bits of a life together, but by spring we both knew this was nothing we could sustain. Emotionally stripped bare, unable to paint, hardly civil to anyone but each other, we either had to make a life together or break it off entirely. Henry knew I would have left everything to be with him: I told him so, flat-out, in the plainest words I knew. And saw the hesitation on his face. Too late, I realized that even with Henry, I should've played the game. Too late,

I recalled my mother's Old World advice: Indifference is the way you hold a man.

The cold April morning we sat at the table, looking out at the rain, he covered my hands with his and said, "It will kill her if I leave." I said, "Rubbish. Eventually, she'll be fine." He was quiet for a while. Then he said, "I'm sorry, Agnes. I have to go."

Six weeks later, I woke one morning and found myself in a new place, knowing neither customs nor language. Leaving Edward asleep in the same bed where I'd first made love with Henry, I made my way down the cool dark hall to my studio. I made a pot of tea, and while it steeped, I mixed paint on the broad glass palette I still use. I stood beside the window as I worked, occasionally glancing up at the smudge-colored sky that would eventually brighten to gray. The city at this hour, in its relative silence, gave me the closest thing I knew to peace. I looked at my reflection in the black glass: angular and plain as always. Seeing myself like that, I knew I continued to exist.

As I lifted my first cup of tea to my lips, a sea of nausea caught me in its undertow. I didn't have to wrinkle my brow, calculate dates, suspect I had the flu. I knew the source immediately, and that the child I'd conceived had not come from my occasional late-night grapplings with Edward.

I worked on the painting, allowing myself to hope that I could—with a single phone call—unravel the exile Henry had placed me in. The May morning I dialed Henry's number in Philadelphia, my only thought was how to keep him on the line—*You must not write, you must not telephone.* When there was no answer, I tried again another hour, then another day, then every day for the best part of a week. Finally I called Blake.

"I assume you know about the fellowship," he said. "He's already left for Paris."

"Paris?" I said weakly.

I hadn't known about the fellowship, but I did know that nothing about a fellowship is instantaneous. He'd applied for it months before, had already won it when he last saw me. It forced his hand: Which one of us would he take to Paris?

We lived in a different age—no cell phones, no email, nothing that could be private in that way between lovers. Blake gave me Henry's address and phone in Paris. His wife answered when I called, and I stumbled out something about a show I was inviting him to be in. A week later, when he still hadn't returned the call, I sent a letter asking him to phone me. As the weeks passed, I felt desperate, then smashed to bits, then angry.

One morning while I was vomiting up my breakfast, Edward called to me from the shower, "Hey, Ags, I think you might be pregnant." And was delighted, at least until the baby came. That he felt no more for her than mild affection knocked the pilings out from under him. His own child, whom he couldn't love. He spent years in therapy over that one.

The next winter, in a black mood, I hunched my shoulders, narrowed my eyes at the icy wind. I hung wet diapers on the line until my fingers chapped, looked down the stretch of brown grass running empty to the windbreak—the overgrown yard of my new home. The same wrists Henry touched his lips against the morning we said goodbye were tired from reaching overhead, clipping white cotton to the line so it could freeze in the crackling wind.

I thought, *He doesn't write, he doesn't telephone, because he keeps the only promise he ever made to me.*

Shivering, I entered the house where our infant daughter slept a few precious hours every afternoon, the only time I could reliably be alone. I lit the burner under the breakfast coffee, bitterness wafted through the room, not even the cup between my cold hands could warm them.

The old chair scraped across the wooden floor, and on the table were newspapers and magazines. Vietnam was everywhere, the grainy photographs showing my suffering for what it was, personal, therefore unimportant. Even young as I was, I knew I was luckier than most: I had my work, I had Rika, in whose round face Henry's blue eyes shone. I had a successful husband, Edward, whose eyes were also blue, but not at all like Henry's, and seemed to narrow with suspicion a little more each day.

That afternoon, if I'd tracked him down in Paris, Henry might have said, "Agnes, what do you want from me?"

I would have said, "This," and listened to him breathe, listened to whatever words he could push across the wire. I would have told a lie, because what I wanted from him was everything. Hearing Henry's voice again, I think I might have shattered.

There's a photo of me, dated May 1974, tall and bony in a dark sweater and jeans, sitting on the bed with Rika, who can't even sit alone. Edward took the picture, which must account for my unbrushed hair, the sea of newspaper on the floor, the lace unraveling from the spread. If something needed repair or was out of place, Edward had the gift of making me see it—a tiresome quality, as it turned out.

If I could point to the thing most out of place in that picture, the thing most desperately in need of repair, it would be me. At thirty-four, I looked a decade older, haggard, shell-shocked, a plume of gray visible in my dark hair. I had some strange sense of nobility, as if by keeping the heartache to myself, I had proof that I could survive anything life would ever throw my way.

Some days in the studio, I painted while Rika screamed in her playpen, and I thought, *This is what a woman does, she picks up the pieces and puts them back together in a semblance of a whole, and if there's something missing, only she knows, and carries on without it, without sympathy, without consolation.* Nothing but the sheer force of her will gets her through each bloody moment, day after day, until the blessed end.

What I didn't know then—work was all I could rely on. When Henry was gone, and then Edward, and even eventually Rika, I still had my painting. I look back on myself in those days with pity, as I still thought love would be what saved me.

Instead, what saved me was standing in front of the canvas day after day after day, even when it was blank. Sometimes I'd do nothing but clean my brushes, terrified that this is all I'd ever be able to do again. The good months—the good years, sometimes when I was lucky—when the work came easily, I thought I'd finally arrived, and that the fallow times were behind me. Eventually I came to see that it's a cycle. Sometimes the work comes steadily, sometimes it's famine or feast, but even when the field is dry and there's no promise of rain, you still have to be out there, staring up at the sky, ready when the first drop falls.

Every love story has a beginning and an end, and that's where the tale is usually focused: What drew the lovers together. What tore the lovers apart. The middle part is only what haunts you at four in the morning, when you lie awake remembering the funny thing he said about his parents, the way he listened to you talk with his eyes fixed on yours and his head cocked to one side. I wondered, if I spent so much time thinking of him, surely mustn't his mind wander occasionally to me?

But to try to weave my own peculiarities into his was undoubtedly a mistake. For years in fact, I didn't understand that if he'd loved me more, he'd have made a different choice. He weighed his options, and my side of the scale came up light. Who ever wants to believe they've been passed over? And knowing it, who ever feels quite the same again?

Mayo lies at my feet, snoring, resigned that her routine's been disrupted for the night. Resignation. Patience. Two qualities not in my original oeuvre. I still have neither in abundance, but if we're put on earth to learn what doesn't come naturally to us, I've had lessons enough for a doctoral degree.

It's past midnight, and I sit by the window, looking over my patch of woods, the barren yard of the 1970s now grown thick with trees. In the stillness, the snow seems a white page on which the lines are drawn, and each line a tree branch.

I pour myself another glass of wine, and look at the name and number written on the pad beside the phone: *Ben Tillman.* How strange, the memory of a voice, the memory of sound. Unheard for decades, yet I knew it instantly. The initial hesitation, almost stuttering the first few words, and then the same light tone and timbre. A voice that dipped easily into irony, at odds with his gentle words. Until Ben spoke to me tonight, I'd forgotten how that irony used to make me feel—closed out, walled off from what Henry was really thinking.

In my lap is the small wooden box where for years I've kept the astrologer's wrinkled paper telling of the life that Henry and I might have shared. So many times I was tempted to send it to him, as if it were proof of something. Henry would've laughed at me for putting faith in hocus-pocus.

"We make our own reality, Agnes," he used to say when I cursed fate or luck. Astrology? I might as well have cited proclamations from the Oracle. Henry might've been touched by my optimism, he might have laughed at my superstition, but mostly, he'd have been annoyed that I hadn't done as he asked: *You must not write or telephone. We have to make a clean break* . . . Because how much easier that was, finally, for him.

The wooden box holds stones, an iron hinge, a shard of broken blue pottery, a button from Henry's black winter coat, an empty cigarette pack folded into a red-and-white square, topped with silver foil. Where did I collect this detritus of our sliced-up life? In the moments between his leaving and my own. Mornings when he was in the shower. Afternoons when we climbed through the evergreen woods, our fingers laced together like two ordinary people with a lifetime opening out ahead of us.

The box contains my silence. It contains the feeling of the cold window I pressed my forehead against the morning I watched him walk down the gravel drive to his car, my last sight of him his palm raised behind a rain-splashed windshield.

Complete idiocy, I think now, not to have opened the door and run outside, and when he stopped the car, told him that by nightfall we could be in Carolina, at his cottage by the sea, where we'd write the necessary letters, make the necessary phone calls that would allow us to begin a life together.

And why not? Many people have done things just as difficult, looked into the eyes of the person they swore they'd spend their one life with and said, *I take it back, I made a mistake, it's someone else I love.* Words that take courage to speak.

Rika was nearly a year old when I ran into Blake at a party for someone up-and-coming in New York. He'd avoided me since the awkwardness about Henry and the fellowship; he was nervous enough about his role in our affair. Edward's reputation as a critic was taking off, and back then I was just another painter.

When Blake saw me walking across the room, his face fell. He said that yes, he'd heard from Henry. After France, he was back in Philadelphia, where he was doing illustration work and a little freelance graphic design.

"Is Lisa with him?" I asked.

"Agnes," he said, as if I'd asked something obvious. "Of course she is. They've been together since they were twelve."

"Are they happy?" I demanded.

"I don't know, I really don't know," he said, lifting his hands apologetically. "It doesn't really seem to make any difference now, does it?"

"Did you tell him I'd had the child?" I demanded.

Blake looked surprised, as if he was just connecting the dots. Then he shook his head and said, "Honestly, Agnes? We didn't even talk about you."

Then Blake died a few years later, and more years passed and people who might have known us both were scarce. People who knew we'd been together were almost nonexistent. I never heard Henry's name at parties, stopped looking for mentions in the journals. He went another way, took a path he saw early on: On the phone tonight, his son said Henry spent his life illustrating and writing children's books. "A life that made him happy."

If this is the path he saw for himself, he must have known how miserable he'd make my life. And in truth, how miserable I would have made his—always pushing him to do what he wasn't passionate about doing. Never a moment's rest . . . just work, and thinking about work, and when that wasn't happening, glancing up to see what trouble Rika had gotten herself into. Would he have let her stand at the studio door, knocking piteously, and not let her in, as I so often did? Or would he have set his work aside, pulled her into his lap, and read to her, drawn with her, talked to her? Had he known about Rika, would he at least have stayed in touch?

Finding me would've been a snap. Bits were splashed all over. Cover stories in all the art glossies. My shows reviewed in *The New Yorker*, my shows reviewed in *The New York Times*. And now that I'm middling sixty, every mark that I make on the page seems to interest someone.

On the phone tonight, for every question I asked, Ben had an answer, and I pasted it in place alongside what I already knew. What I'd imagined wrongly, I covered up with new bits of information.

"How's your mother?" I asked, the concerned family friend.

"Good," he said. "She's good. She came to the funeral."

"Your parents divorced?"

"Long time ago," he said. "Mom left when I was twelve, and well—I stayed with my dad."

Mom left: Lisa, the fragile one who couldn't have survived alone. So simple after all, to leave. I wanted to ask for the particulars—why she left, how Henry had reacted—but Ben was already telling me how late, late, in Henry's life, there was another wife, much younger, and a baby girl . . . "Some real happiness at last," he said.

I didn't say much of anything as I sat listening, but what I thought was how different for a woman: no chance to start over at sixty with a young husband. On the other hand, at sixty, a woman has already raised her children. Who would choose to go through that pain again?

Ben said, "My dad and I used to talk about your work all the time. When I was in art school I'd bring home books, and we'd go through them together. He loved the paintings. But he never said he knew you until I visited him at Christmas, and he gave me this letter to mail after he'd passed away."

After.

Somehow, the sound of it sliced me to the core. When I found my voice, what I meant to ask was "Why after?" but what came out was, "Why you?"

I could almost hear him shrug. "Dad said the letter was important and . . . ," he laughed nervously, "he'd haunt me if I didn't get it to you. He knew I'd take him seriously."

"You believe in ghosts," I said.

"I believe in my father," he said.

I listened to his silence opening a space for me to walk to. Finally, I said, "We were lovers."

"I figured that." Ben's voice soothed in a way I knew well. "He cared for you a lot. I could tell by the way he talked."

I leaned my forehead against the cold window. For a moment, the color and texture and temperature and taste of being with Henry was so keen, his death seemed as unreal as the years since I'd last touched him. What I wanted his son to understand was not the beginning of our love, nor the way it ended. I wanted to share the core of it, elusive and ineffable even as I heard myself begin to speak.

"We had a handful of beautiful, gray afternoons and mornings, some frozen midnights. You should have seen the way the snow filled the trees. He forgot his gloves and his hands were chapped. We walked the woods like children, picking up stones, tree bark, whatever looked interesting. He knew what everything was called, every tree and plant, every creature. And after . . . ,"

I paused, uncertain where my thoughts were going to take me. I could say that after, I lived my life as if it were real and full of purpose. I could say that after, I knew my life was a shadow of what it could have been. And the sheer ribbon of black ice between these truths was where I balanced. It's where I balance still.

On the other end of the line, Ben waited. The silence stretched out past awkwardness. He was giving me time to pull myself together. He was good at this. I remembered Henry, patiently waiting for me to calm down after he said he wouldn't see me, waiting for me to realize that our time together was already at an end.

"Ben?" I said.

"I'm here," he said gently.

I sat up straight and looked back at myself from the window glass, white-haired, white-faced, the black receiver cupped against my ear. I held onto it with both hands.

"Dear heart," I said, "can you understand this? At the moment, I wish he'd never been born."

Agnes Landowska:
Her Life and Art

1. Woman in White

Julia sat in a room that she first saw in a magazine. The caption beneath the photograph had read, *Edward Brooks relaxes in the living room of his Manhattan apartment.* Her professor, the noted art critic, a young maverick, sat in the chair before the open door; only the edges and corners of paintings and furniture intruded into the black and white shot.

The professor spent every Christmas vacation in Rome and this year had arranged for Julia to be the hired presence meant to deter theft. While he nibbled gnocchi in a little restaurant off the Corso, Julia sat cross-legged on his velvet sofa, sipping burgundy from a glass so thin she was afraid to set it down. The French doors to the terrace were locked. Orange twilight settled over the copper roof of the bank across Fifth, lit the stone and copper of the buildings all the way to the river, which she could not see. She was waiting for her lover, though she knew he was unlikely to arrive.

She looked around at the spruce-colored walls, the parquet floor, the kilim, the cold fireplace, and behind glass, on the dark-stained shelves, rows and rows of books, many inscribed by their authors. Most particularly, she looked at the wall where the woman's portrait hung. Looking mildly outward like a patron saint who never expected adulation, bare-breasted, white-gowned, the woman cupped her hands in her lap and wore a look of waiting, neither patient nor impatient, happy nor sad.

Julia was fairly sure this was her professor's ex-wife, the one that the students whispered about. And so she practiced her look. She closed her eyes and tried to imagine herself as a portrait, but it was no use. Who would paint her, in her glasses, with her imperfect breasts and a face that hid nothing? If she were a painter, she would paint herself sitting in this lovely room, slowly getting drunk on the eve of another year. She would paint without embellishment or self-pity, with bold strokes, in dull, accurate colors.

All afternoon she had been reading Chekhov, whose books were not inscribed but were heavily underlined, in pencil, by her absent host. According to Chekhov, every woman believes she is the unhappiest person alive.

Julia took another sip of burgundy and wondered how it was possible for a man to understand this, if perspective granted him insight, or long experience. She thought of Chekhov, with his pince-nez and sad eyes, listening to the heart of the woman in the painting on the opposite wall. At his ear he held an old-fashioned stethoscope and did not even glance at her bare breasts, round and tawny as goblets full of chardonnay. In her cotton dress, she looked to be a creature from a warmer region, while he was pale and thin under his scratchy woolen underwear. The woman stared over his head, implacable, her hands in her lap open and empty.

"Ah," he sighed, and straightened to look her in the eye. He'd heard the locus of her trouble, a small pellet lodged between her magnificent breasts. Unhappiness. Yes. He studied her face, and the gray eyes that once seemed indifferent now smoldered with the myrrh of unhappiness.

Julia looked at the painting closely. The woman's white dress had not slipped casually from her shoulders; instead, the cotton folds bunched tightly around her elbows, pinning her arms to her sides. The sun angled in over Chemical Bank, slanting across the painting and flooding the green room with golden, moted light. Maybe this was the point of the white dress: a final salvo before the ex-wife walked out the door. She'd lived here, the other students said: Her studio had been in one of the bedrooms.

The previous night Julia and her lover walked the empty streets from the subway station to this building, unlocked the double doors and took the listing, trembling elevator to the top floor. They switched on lights, laid a fire in the fireplace, ate a meal of pasta, bread, and wine. In the morning he took the IRT back uptown, where he changed clothes and vacuumed his apartment. Around noon, he took a bus out to the airport, and met his wife as she descended the jet way into the Eastern Airlines terminal.

As Julia stood at the door with him that morning, he put his lips against the skin beneath her right ear and whispered, "I will see you if I can."

Chilling words, for translated into the language of realism, they meant "I will not be able to get away."

Julia told herself that she was nobody's fool, but in fact this was the man she hoped to marry. In October, standing in Riverside Park, she'd looked into his face and understood with a pang like a hot spike under her ribs the paramount cliché of romantic movies and pop songs: Destiny. For all its sibilance, it had an ugly sting.

Why didn't you wait for me? she wanted to ask him. *Didn't you know I'd be here?*

In Rome, where it was nearly midnight, her absent host and his current lover filled their mouths with champagne. The woman leaned shakily against the man's arm and said, "Let's call home!" because it seemed a little odd, to be so far from the city where she had celebrated so many nights like this one, though never with this particular man.

Already a little bored by the woman's relentless optimism, her attempts to inject gaiety into the most mundane occasions (buying a newspaper, clipping one's toenails), the professor agreed and dialed the one number he knew by heart, which happened to be his own.

Julia made her way across the room, still holding the delicate glass, leaned her head against the barred window, and spoke into the receiver: ". . . Yes, everything's fine. The weather's lovely—cold but no snow . . . , Don't worry, I found an extra blanket in the hall closet . . . No, I'm staying in tonight . . . no plans . . . so many drunks on the streets . . . Do you think so? . . . All right . . . Happy New Year to you, too . . . All right . . . I will . . . Good-bye."

She took a mouthful of wine and twisted her fingers through her hair, which was curly and red, "the color of saffron," her professor had written in the curious note he left on the bedside table beside the extra key.

She thought of his face, of his lips against the receiver, of his words traveling over the cold black ocean to reach the smooth pink cave of her ear. Tonight she would sleep in his bed, perhaps the bed he'd once shared with the woman in the painting. She'd slide between sheets he had tucked around the mattress. She shivered, looked into the face of the portrait on the opposite wall, and touched her own breast, which tingled under her palm. Yes, she thought. *I see what you see is about to happen.*

Out the window, on the opposite side of the street were bank employees, workers from the sweatshops, stenographers, the illegal aliens from the coffee shop on the corner: She counted them off as they hurried past with their hands in their coat pockets, scurrying away from the silent, shadowy cavern this street became at nightfall. She sat on top of the mahogany desk beside the window, and put her bare feet in the leather chair.

Duraflame logs lay beside the fireplace, a neat stack with a note in her professor's precise hand urging her to *Feel free to use.* Julia remembered reading somewhere that in New York City, a cord of wood cost hundreds of dollars. She thought of this now, unaccountably, remembering all the cords of wood she had helped her father stack against the garage of the house where her mother still lived. When they finished, the split logs hid the clapboards so completely, from one perspective the garage looked to be made of logs. They had laughed at that, standing out in the weather, waiting for her mother to call them in for supper. She thought her father knew what there was to know about stacking wood. It was years later, after he died, and Julia and her mother worked down to the last layer of logs, that they saw how termites had riddled the siding.

The woman with bared breasts stared back at her, across a room quickly emptying of light. Julia moved her feet across the leather chair, thinking *His chair, this is where he works, this is where I will put my hands on his shoulders and he'll turn around, surprised . . .*

She poured more wine into the thin glass. From the shadows came a sound like a cough, dry and cautionary. It was the ancient radiator, or death itself stealing into the picture.

How am I to know what will happen? Julia thought, coiling her hair around one finger.

She tilted her glass and drank to duplicity, to her fear of the singular pronoun, and then to the women who have waited in fading light for love's arrival, knowing that the hardest hours are yet to come.

2. Rika in Black Glass

At four-thirty on a December afternoon, Agnes sat playing the piano. She had been playing for several hours and her hands were tired; occasionally she rubbed them together, then flexed the long, chapped fingers. She closed her eyes and relaxed her shoulders, which tended to cramp when she played the piano. She sat with her hands in her lap, breathing deeply, and thought about the difficult notes she had not played well. If she could only reach further into herself, she would play those notes, but, she reasoned, *self* was lately a great frozen tundra, and who wanted to embark on such a journey?

Into this pause drifted sounds from elsewhere in the house. Her daughter was with her for the holidays this year and had turned on the radio. From where she sat, the noise sounded like a conversation between two people in a distant room: a man's voice, then a woman's, then the man's again. Then music, and more conversation—a talk show or the news. The piano stood in one corner of the living room—a cheerful place with a tawny leather sofa and many books in tall, white bookshelves. The blond wood floor felt chilly.

She rubbed her feet together, in blue wool socks, and shook her big hands in the air. Then she opened her eyes and played a few, tentative chords on the piano. No, it was no good—she was tired now and might as well give it up for the day.

She shuffled the pages of her music and laid them to one side but continued sitting at the piano with her hands on her lap. Beyond the piano was a wall of bare windows. Outside, snow was falling, piling up on the black branches.

Agnes sat very straight and still on the piano bench. Small birds swooped around the feeders she had placed in the birches, snatching seeds to take them through the long, cold night. These were the birds that didn't migrate; she grew so used to them picking through the spilled millet, it was possible to see them and not to see them at the same time. Juncos and sparrows blew about like leaves, but there were cardinals, too, the scarlet males and their drab-bodied life-mates waiting in the silver web of birches, then swooping in to rifle the grain.

As the light waned the birds flew to farther branches; at some point, which Agnes always looked for and missed, they disappeared until morning.

That it was possible to feel despair in such beautiful surroundings seemed to Agnes an obscenity she was forever repenting. When she was growing up in a tiny apartment that smelled of incense, cabbage, and her parents' bodies, despair seemed as natural as shoes. She rarely saw birds in the stunted trees of her gray, industrial birthplace—the official story was that the birds carried a rare disease, and that was why they'd been destroyed. But of course there was no disease. They were destroyed because they were free. They could not be controlled, or regulated, or told where to go.

Did she really remember the nets, the sacks of poisoned grain, the bodies of dead birds scooped from the sidewalks by women with scarves knotted beneath their chins and aprons tied over their drab coats, or did those images come later, when her face was no longer pressed against the drafty windows overlooking the Boulevard of the Heroes of the Revolution?

Perhaps they flew from a passage in Bach's difficult concerto, across three fleeting chords in an allegro by Shostakovich, into a painting she made while listening to music.

Agnes closed the keyboard. Perhaps the images fluttered into a shadowy crevice of her brain at the Institute of Music on the morning when, barely into her teens, she realized that she would never be more than a competent pianist and had better prepare for another kind of life.

She turned her hands indifferently, examining them: strong, short-nailed. Thick, blue veins roped across the branched tendons, under skin dry and almost imperceptibly freckled. A painter's hands. On the palms, deep lines traced divergences, quirks of fate, indecision in the cross-hatching: Somewhere in there, she had always been a painter. If she knew where to look she could find her departure from her homeland, the moment when the doors of the train opened in Paris, and when the plane landed in New York, and the miles of road since then. One fine line was Edward, etched into the spiderweb that was their marriage, and another, the line she'd walked away from him. Rika's father was a broader line, cut across her palm like a scar. Her daughter grew across a lateral, the spiny link between her heart and life. It was a burden, really, knowing that even her death lay upon her palm like a faint blue shadow.

Evening had already gathered in the corners of the room, but here in front of the windows, the room was lit by falling snow. When Agnes heard footsteps on the stairs she did not turn around, though she knew Rika paused behind her.

Agnes had been silent so long, her voice came out in a croak. "What are you listening to?"

"Nothing."

"Are you ready for dinner?"

She heard the girl's shrug, her stubborn silence, a shift of weight from foot to foot, demanding her mother's attention.

"Are you hungry?"

Rika sighed. "I don't know."

"How can you not know?" Agnes turned around.

Rika stood beside the newel post with her arms folded, leaning against it in what was now near darkness. Rika, her only child, fifteen and morose. Here she dangled on her own slender thread over the threshold of womanhood, a composition, a complex figure inventing the space around it.

Stubborn as your father, Agnes thought. *And, by the way, calculated aloofness bores me to death.*

Rika shrugged again, unfolding herself from her pose. One hand swooped up to flick the light switch on. "Why are you sitting here in the dark?" the girl said, wiping her hair back from her face with both hands.

Agnes put her hand against her eyes, blinking in the sudden brightness. "Birds," she said, turning back to the window, and in the instant defined as inspiration, saw her daughter opening her wings across a landscape of black glass.

3. The Open Window

Ah, Edward said, stepping back from the window. *Of course—we've been away all summer. She's used to the house being empty.*

He angled himself behind the edge of Belgian lace curtain and continued to stare at the bare shoulders and back of the woman next door. Lesley, her name was. They'd spoken a few times in the spring, on the weekends when he was reading in his chair on the lawn and she was working in her garden. The houses here in the old part of town were only a few feet apart.

This morning she was rummaging through a dresser drawer. Her hair hung in wet coils that separated over the pale knobs of her shoulders. Around her waist, she'd tied a blue-and-white-striped towel.

Like a man, Edward thought. *Strange that she doesn't cover her breasts, as if they don't even matter.*

When Julia got out of the shower, she pulled on the panties and bra she'd taken into the bathroom and covered herself with a thick pink terry-cloth robe.

Of course, he considered, *we have children. Boys. Teenagers.*

He shook his head. To think that a man of his age would still have children around; most of his friends were free of their offspring now, settled into a quiet life with their books and their wives and their paid-off mortgages. He loved his sons but longed for the solitude that would come only in their absence. He wished them a speedy adolescence, good schools, a pleasant and independent life.

He'd wished the same for the pale, sulky daughter of his first marriage, but who knew if she'd achieved it? Rika had a child of her own now, whom he'd never seen, and when he called on Christmas and her birthday, she spoke grudgingly, reluctant to part with the details of her life.

As if I haven't the right to ask, Edward thought, and as always, willed himself to think of something else.

He sipped his coffee. With Julia at work and his two sons back in school, he'd come up to his study to work in blessed silence. Instead, he'd found his attention concentrated on one triangle of Lesley's room, the space between the window and the wall, an area of only a few square feet. The white curtains in the long window facing his house framed the scene: Against the wall stood the dresser, an old piece made of dark oak, with Victorian scrollwork.

This wasn't the first time he'd noticed the room. One afternoon as he reached for a book from his bookcase, he glanced down and saw the dresser through the window, and on it a blue-and-white Chinese vase, probably bought at an import store. Still, he admired the way it looked sitting on the dresser alone, like a museum piece. From a distance, everything looked valuable and well-kept.

He liked having people again in the house next door. The old woman who'd lived there when they moved out from the city had finally died last fall, just as the cold was settling in. Though he got used to seeing blank, yellowed window shades staring back at him from the windows, and the realtor's sign weathering in the yard all winter, the emptiness depressed him. In April, the sign disappeared from the yard, and two women moved in. Filmy white curtains replaced the yellowed shades. At night, he could see lamplight through the drawn curtains, and sometimes shapes as the women moved about the rooms. In daylight, when the curtains were open, he sometimes watched patches of sunlight crawl across the wood floors.

Lesley, he thought. *And . . . ?*

He couldn't think of the other woman's name. He rarely saw her. She left for work early, in her rusting Toyota. In the evening, she drove her car up the alley and into the gravel drive. The garage door opened ,as if she'd waved a magic wand at it, and swallowed her car. She entered the house from the garage. He'd met her once, back in June, before he and his family left for Rome. She told him her name and looked him square in the eye, short and plump, with spiky black hair and wrinkles fanned around her eyes, dark as coffee beans. She looked like someone who spent a lot of time outdoors, but only Lesley worked in their yard. Edward had instantly disliked her and tried to compensate by being overly polite. He saw by her slight smirk that he hadn't fooled her.

"What do you think about those two next door?" he'd asked his wife after he came in from talking with them.

"I don't think anything, because I am too damned busy taking care of my own business," Julia answered, her voice so flat and hard, he was reluctant to say more.

He'd gone upstairs to his study, chastened. In the old days, Julia would have smiled while he speculated endlessly about the domestic arrangements next door. Now he stood at the window, coffee cup in hand. Who would have thought their marriage—begun in such passion, fifteen years difference in their ages, mildly scandalous because she'd been his student—would turn out like this? Julia hardly bothered to look up from her boxes of slides when he dropped hints about a woman he'd slept with. Sometimes her indifference made him suspect that he'd reached a point in his life where his lovers acquiesced simply to indulge him. Fucking him was a rite of passage, like taking comps and defending the dissertation.

But he pushed that idea aside. The women always cried too hard when he broke it off, telling them that his wife had discovered the affair and threatened to strip him of his sons, his house, his Mercedes, all that he held dear. He could see himself now, holding the woman's head against his chest, wiping at her tears, his gestures gone suddenly paternal. As he held her close, breathing in her smell, he felt stirrings of longing that were surprisingly devoid of lust. He wanted to carve himself onto the woman's history, know that he'd had a hand in shaping the person she'd grow up to be. He wanted her adoration, and in all but a few cases, he'd gotten it. He'd stayed friends with most of his former lovers, recommending them for jobs, publishing their papers, sometimes even speaking at their weddings. One woman had named her son after him; another called her daughter Brooke, a sly move he appreciated. Neither child was his, of course. He wouldn't have appreciated that gesture.

Lesley closed her dresser drawer and placed small white garments beside the Chinese vase: a bit of lace, a thin strap, a triangle of silk. She opened the hinged lid of a small, wooden jewelry box, stirred through the contents with one finger before fishing out her earrings.

Edward felt his pulse quicken as he watched her turn her head to one side, face away from the window, and thread the thin wire of the earring through the tiny hole in her left ear lobe. Her hair swept across her back, baring one milky shoulder. She stood as if deep in thought, her hands motionless at her ear.

He wondered if she was listening to the radio, as Julia did in the mornings when she dressed for work. He'd long since stopped complaining about the intrusion of strangers' voices into his morning calm, tried to tune out the rapid-fire delivery of disaster and traffic and weather that goaded his family out the door.

"I don't have time to read the paper," Julia reminded him in an accusatory voice, making him feel guilty, though he wasn't sure why. He liked to get up early, before the rest of the family, put on the first of two or three pots of coffee he'd drink that day, and shake out the *Times* on the dining-room table. Reading made a calm pool in the turbulent river of morning, and he awakened gradually over the neat columns of newsprint. Then at seven, Julia's alarm brayed, and her feet thumped onto the floor over his head. She and the boys slammed doors and gulped Pop-Tarts and raced up and down the stairs while he cowered behind the paper, barely catching their muttered goodbyes as they departed for lives in which he figured minutely, if at all.

Lesley slowly lowered her hands to her sides. She was a thin, lovely woman in her thirties, someone who seemed to be on loan from an earlier century. He'd thought this the first time he saw her coming out of her house in a long, gauzy skirt, in a flowing blouse, with that ridiculous straw hat on her head. He could hardly admit what she reminded him of, but today, he knew: the portrait he'd had to sell years ago, when he could no longer afford the insurance.

The skin of her arms and shoulders had the same translucent glow Agnes's had above the open bodice of the white dress he'd bought for her in Tuscany, when they were newly married. Near the end, in an act of perversity, she'd painted herself in it as if it were an instrument of torture—the low neckline shoved down until it pinned her arms to her sides. Her flat-gray eyes stared out, expressionless as her dark nipples. She seemed empty of everything, even hope, and the jaunty fullness of her breasts mocked him.

For years, as he lay before the fire shoving himself into the warm wetness of whatever comfort he was mining, he kept his eyes riveted on Agnes's impassive face. *I was faithful to you,* he told her silently, gripping the plush buttocks, stroking the silky head, mouthing the soft breasts.

I was faithful to you, and still, you weren't happy.

In his memory now, Agnes was caught between being a real woman and a painting. He couldn't think of one without immediately conjuring the other. When he'd seen her last, years ago at Rika's wedding, she greeted him like a friendly stranger. He wanted to push her down right there behind the refreshment tent, shove her dress up, and work himself between her thighs, stare into her cool eyes, and ask her what had made him so unsatisfactory. In the end, he hadn't been sorry to let the painting go. A collector in Toronto owned it now, someone who could sit beneath Agnes's unwavering gaze and not feel himself judged.

He rubbed a forefinger across his lips, remembering how she had felt against his skin when he pulled the white dress from her shoulders and laid kisses across her back. He stared out the window at where Lesley stood without moving. Across her shoulders fell a rich, tangled blanket of hair. He knew its smell would be woodsy and herbal, still damp as ferns in a deep forest. He imagined his hands buried in it, digging into the soft, springy mass that fell away from either side of her face, and that face lifting to meet his: a dusting of copper freckles across her nose, and her eyes wide-set, the lashes almost transparent, the irises blue and trusting.

She had blue eyes? Edward looked down into them, two startled eyes a dozen feet away. She was laughing, lifting her hands into the air to give him an elaborate, comical shrug that made her small breasts bob. She shook her head at her own thoughtlessness, shook her hair down over her shoulders. She made a wry face as she mouthed the word *Sorry!* and reached up to yank the curtains closed.

He lifted the coffee mug to his lips, staring at the covered window. He let his eyes slide past the house, to the trees that ringed the garden.

Cunt, he muttered.

He took a sip of his coffee, and made himself stand there casually for a moment longer before turning back to what had become his life.

4. Irises

Confined to his hotel by rain on the sixth of February 1912, Matisse wrote to his daughter, "I have begun a bouquet of blue irises."

A hundred years later, in my own old age, I wake to rain, and blue irises nodding in a blue vase on my bedside table. I wake to gray depths in the lace at the window, a gray cat curled into the hollow of my knees, pain pulsing through my shoulder where I have lain still too long. From somewhere in the house comes the tap-tap-tapping of a dry vine against cold glass. The hand against my face smells of turpentine. My hair spreads like a silver pelt beneath my cheek. I flex all the fingers of both hands.

In a room down the hall, my exiled granddaughter murmurs to her infant son. She fears his cry splintering the darkness, as if sound will set objects into motion, make dust float from the untouched floor.

A mindful guest, she fears waking me, but I am past disturbance. Sometimes they fall asleep together and I push the door open to sketch the infant closed in concentrated, passionate rest, his mother curled around him like the exhausted child she still is.

I put my fingers to my eyes and view the world in fragments. I turn my head and look at different corners of the room. The wet, holy hours of early morning tremble through the slice of air slipping over the sill. I sniff it, lifting my head from the feather pillow. The cat pushes against me with all his sleek mechanism of integument and bone. Water courses in the gutters of the house. It's the ending of a season.

I begin a bouquet of blue irises in the blue vase on the bedside table. Behind them, a wall the color of morning, of pale terra-cotta warmed by sun. I sit by the window in a room buffeted by rain. Younger, I waited for the perfect light, a certain heft of shadow. Now I compose with what I find before me, thrifty cook whose soup contains whatever is at hand. Still in my nightgown, the bed unmade, the cat burrowed in the comforter, I set down lines on a white field, the blue trace-work of veins.

The unobservant see flowers as restful, without conflict or emotion. The faces of flowers differ from human faces chiefly in their sameness. One iris looks much like another, saturated blue, and the dependent lip with its yellow oval, like a golden word poised there, waiting to be plucked by a sympathetic ear.

Sometimes the irises whisper into my ear, their troubles surprisingly ordinary. They have issues with sustenance. They feel the water at their stems growing fetid and murky. They sense the first slackness in their petals' thin, elastic skin, heralding the onset of a gradual browning. The color, too, begins to fade the moment the petals unfurl. Near the end, the irises are almost lavender with longing for the indigo of their first hours. Remember us, they plead, at our most beautiful.

Beauty, I tell them, is terrifying when you see—as you inevitably will—what lies beneath it. Beauty is in your imperfection, the detail that gives you some distinction from each other. The blue trace-work laid down on canvas, I think of my great-grandson's skull and the trembling depression where my thumb seeks out his pulse. My hand once lay like that over my daughter's skull when she took my nipple into her mouth and closed her eyes. I stroked her hair and thought about her father, gone for months before her birth.

Giving birth, my granddaughter screamed into my face, she gripped my hand so hard I thought the yellow bones might begin to fuse, she bled, and shit, and beat her fist against the luminous blue paper crackling beneath her. Her hair snarled against her forehead and her face gleamed in the unrelenting light of the delivery room. Sixteen years old, Sara did not look beautiful with her legs held open by the chrome stirrups, her bulging vagina the color of a plum and matted brown pubic hair wet with the amniotic gush. I thought, *Why not paint her this way? Isn't this as real as those tender profiles with the baby at the breast, or stripped to the waist, washing at a tin basin?*

After the birth, I painted Sara from memory like a fierce, raging animal, her body focused in purple concentration as her son's wizened, crimson face emerged between her thighs. And in the composition, she became line and its relationship to color, a stack of triangles, a surface struck by a diagonal of light. Beautifully accurate in its abstraction. Abstractly beautiful in its accuracy.

In the weeks afterward, the slender girl tucking a strand of hair behind her ear and averting her eyes when she spoke became another composition. Bathing her son at the kitchen sink, Sara became fractured light playing over the window. With her silk hair and delicate wrist bones, she has seemed to me all winter very slightly unreal as she grows from her mother's child into this child's mother. On the phone to her lover, she's a wash of chilly light, a paler hue than when she stands in brown confusion speaking to her mother. Her arms are smudges of paint: She opens them, and I can enter at any point, walk her to the borders of the canvas.

In the room down the hall, she sings the song I sang to Rika mornings when I needed sleep and my husband was already typing in his study behind the closed door. I would not allow myself to think of anything but the child cradled in my arms—not the man who'd helped me make her, not even myself, trembling on the edge of desolation.

I didn't dare think of who I'd become, my heart shriveled to a bone, my body aching, the days of constant longing that I couldn't believe had become my life. For months, I pondered reasons for my existence. I might as well have asked, *Why weather? Why night? Why that color in the sky?*

That winter I committed myself to canvas, alone, not "Mother and Child" as everyone no doubt expected, but a bold self-portrait, the last truly figurative work in my whole long oeuvre. Every stroke of the brush seemed a needle under the skin, the fragile cover of a body sodden with betrayal. I stilled my hands upon my lap, bared my breasts, hummed complicated adagios that remained inside my head long after I'd walked through the open door.

I released my childhood birds, walked down the nightmare staircase. Finally, I entered a room half-filled with snow and found a place there. I fixed my gaze unceasingly on the viewer, and when I stepped back, I saw that I'd painted not myself, but the space that had been hollowed out inside me.

It was like breathing for the first time. I found a place to put the evergreen wood I'd glimpsed from a train, the blue gate in my grandmother's village, the yellow nails of my mother's gnarled feet. In came the bird with the crimson eye and the ivory keys I'd used to capture its voice, lacking one of my own. I let despair settle itself in cobalt, turn into moonlight over the fields, a river aimed at the horizon. Where I expected nothing, I found cerulean, ochre, viridian. I found the space endlessly unfolding.

This morning I dip my brush and paint irises the color of milk-breath, with my own gold-flecked eye peering from every flower. I build a room around the flowers, a garden in the walls, myself into a memory. I wash away the surface, make room for other lives. I take my life into my hands. I begin again.

5. Interview

Before she was really known, my mother painted a self-portrait. This was nothing new. Artists have been painting self-portraits since Lascaux, but something about my mother's portrait drew attention in a way her other work hadn't. It was the seventies, for one thing—about the same time, Alice Neel put herself on canvas fat and old and naked, somebody else filmed herself pulling a scroll out of her cooch. "The body" was hot. Mother's painting marked the end of her figurative phase, but it gave her the launch she needed. When I was small, and I'd visit Edward in the city, the painting hung over the fire. I must have been eight or nine when he sold it, and for years afterward, I was absolutely furious at him. She was my mother: How could he not have offered it to me?

Even after I got old enough to understand what insurance was, I was still pissed. She was my mother: I thought she belonged to me. I'd never really reasoned out why Edward had it in the first place. Christ, I was a kid—I thought he kept it because he loved her. It took me a long time to understand, that Agnes left it behind as a kind of grand *fuck you*.

What kind of mother was she? Well, much kinder than you might imagine. She had these arcane skills—I wore dresses with rows of hand-tucked ruching. She sewed them from bedspreads, but they were exquisite. She liked to walk in the woods, and sometimes I tagged along. She taught me a lot about nature, including the human kind. I was forty before I learned that I wasn't conceived in matrimony. She hauled it out like it was some big secret, though I'd always kind of known. She got so furious when I laughed at her, she actually slapped me.

She was dead before I understood why she'd gotten so angry. She'd carried this around for so long, and in some ways, let it define her. To herself, I mean—it had nothing to do with that formidable public face. When I laughed, it was like the great weight she'd been carrying turned out to be sand instead of gold dust.

And the one thing she couldn't abide was being thought trivial. That this might not be unique to her—that's something I'm not sure she ever grasped. My god. Suggesting she was just an ordinary woman? That's really something she wouldn't have heard.

6. Agnes Landowska: Self-Portrait

Cigarettes and coffee, and on slow days, the dust of remembered places: The people who pass here give off these smells, and I take them in like nourishment, until I'm sure my bones are ash, my blood a black river. Inez, the ancient guard, leans against the wall, rubs her nose against her shoulder. She ventures into morning before most people wake, creeps into January's muddy thaw so she can watch the watchers tracking up floors she doesn't have to clean. I love the amber of her bent neck, the white flecks on the shoulders of her black uniform. On slow days, sometimes she dances around the room, or gives me her confessions. She trusts me more than she trusts anyone; I know how to keep a secret.

It's barely light. I rest my legs on the chair's edge and hold my head in line with my cupped hands: a woman sitting half-naked in a chair, waiting for what? I used to know, but in this room my presence is supposed to fill, objectives matter less and less each year. Days pass when no one looks my way except Inez, or else they look so hard I know I'm just a point of focus, a place to vent their worry. The lovelorn. The lonely. I stare into their eyes and think *There's nothing I can say.*

Turned out of their lives I enter my own, a room that smells of turpentine, a space inside my head that seems to shrivel by the year. I study my footprints marking the warp and weave of the unprimed canvas. I thread myself into intimate associations with the brushwork, drink a draught of thinner, learn tension from the stretcher bars, balance from the palette knife's blunt edge. I'm the product of one sad winter of a woman's life. She rubbed salt into my pigments, entrusted me with a sorrow she could never bring herself to speak. I was a problem to be solved, and she solved it. I was obsolete the moment she laid the brush aside.

She painted me into a corner, one dust-webbed angle of a room, the one closest to the window, for light is what she wanted, the gray light of early morning, the cold light of snowfall. Light blooms silver on my chest, rose against my lap, ochre where my shoulder meets the wall. Light washes my face, reducing me to charcoal line and scumbled glaze. The day will move through me like an instrument of grace, plucking details that make me seem more than a seated figure, that give me heart, soul, an after-life imprinted on the retina like a half-remembered dream.

Look at it this way: I should have something to say for myself at last, should become more than cool, flat planes of color as I watch the ones who move inside these walls like shadows in a dream. All I was ever willed to be is an interpretation of emptiness. *Yes,* they say, their eyes upon my face, *this is how it feels.* The light moves around the room. Inez unfolds herself from her corner like a great black crow, rushing visitors from our room, directing them to an exhibition of Chinese porcelain in the main gallery. She turns in the sudden quiet and says, "Honey, you won't believe what happened to me last night . . . ," grimaces and shakes her head.

I half-expect my hands to flutter from my lap and take her by the elbows. *Yes*, I think. *I know what happened.*

Because it is what always happens. Someone dares to love. She stands before me, a narrative in her posture, a color to her life, a line around her feelings. When our eyes meet, I speak to her, my voice like a bird's song floating through the trees, looping over branches. The bird itself is invisible.

Taken

Rika Pratt, the poet, is sitting in the Colony garden before supper, a cool and windless April afternoon, her worn red notebook open across her lap. At the top of a blank page, she's written *peonies* in her tiny, looping cursive, having seen the early nubs of the peony plant emerging from the ground. And then: Almost sexual. Firm rosy fingers pushing through matted grass, an early sign of spring.

She probes until she finds another plant, and another, a whole bed of peonies growing beside the concrete bench. No trace yet of the firm, green stalk, the tough leaves, the tightly wrapped bud of the eventual flower. Bright-pink shoots, tender as silk—and yet how hardy the plant must be, since the nights here still dip below freezing.

As she reaches down to pull away the old growth, a splinter of woody stalk punctures the skin of her right hand. "Damn," she says, fumbling at the splinter left-handedly, succeeding only in driving it deeper.

"Hello!" someone calls, and she turns to look over her shoulder. One of the painters is loping across the grass, coming in from the woods. Ben. Young, bearded, blond, he smiles as he approaches, backpack swinging from his shoulder.

"What've you got there?"

She holds out her hand. "A splinter," she says.

He leans over her, lifts her hand, and in a few seconds, gently scrapes away the sliver of stalk.

"Thanks," she says, feeling awkward as he stands there, smiling faintly and saying nothing, squinting a little in the late-afternoon sun.

She says, "I got it from the peonies," and turns to pull back the matted grass and broken stalks, exposing the ruby shoots.

Ben crouches beside her. "My dad told me a folk tale once about a woman who found a mushroom growing in her garden. When she pulls it, turns out it's the ear of a witch."

He smiles and looks at Rika, who's radiant with the delight of being in the garden—for just a moment, she's a young girl sitting there in her long, brown skirt and blue sweater, hair in a bun against her neck.

Rika looks up from the peonies in time to catch a flicker of something on Ben's face as he looks at her—a tenderness that starts in his eyes. In the week they and a dozen others have been in residence at the Colony, they've had a few conversations about the wildlife around the place, the trails he's walked. He seems hardly more than a boy, with the blithe confidence of someone who's always been the prize student, not yet slapped down by the world.

She remembers the feeling in herself, that success was a matter of course. Everyone knew she was brilliant. Gifted. So early on, who could see that what she lacked was the ruthlessness to put her poems above all else? Thirty-four now, she's settled for less than she expected, though she imagines this is true of most people. Still, she hopes that someday soon, she'll stop feeling like she's waiting for her life to begin.

Ben says, "Maybe I'll come back tomorrow and draw this," and Rika pieces the story together—the backpack slung over one shoulder, he's been out sketching in the woods. As he gets to his feet and waits for her to collect her things (she's been in the garden all afternoon, writing), she's aware of the energy in his body, a restlessness that seems to propel him at a different speed from her own. As they make their way along the grass path through the garden and up the back steps to the main house, where dinner will soon be served, Rika thinks, *Probably in school he played sports. There's something decisive about his walk.*

At table, he takes the chair beside hers. Passing the serving bowls, they're close enough that she can smell him, a scent she associates with children at play. With nervous fingers, Rika pleats the napkin in her lap, listening as he tells a story. In the woods this afternoon, he saw a grouse, he thinks, because later he heard the drumming of its wings.

Rika's the only one at the table who's ever seen a grouse, but when he describes the bird, he speaks to her directly. She looks down at her plate, and when she looks back, he's still watching her. At first, she thinks she's imagining things—she's used to being invisible, the quiet one easy to pass over—but when it happens again, and then again, Rika feels a blush creep up her neck and flood her face. With her blood humming, she feels compelled to hold his gaze, as if looking away might sever a connection suddenly forged between them. In this light, his eyes seem almost navy blue.

And then he says, "Rika, tell them what you found in the garden," and her hand trembles, making coffee jump from her cup onto the white tablecloth. As she fumbles with words to explain the peonies (unsexing them, no reason to share what she thought with this group of relative strangers), Ben lays his napkin over the stain spreading across the tablecloth, a gesture so kind and quick and careful, she feels herself falling for him right there.

Mopping the coffee stain is a reflex from the half-dozen years Ben spent waiting tables, paying his way through art school (for although he has the look of a prep-school boy, his father was also an artist, his mother's a teacher, and he's used to scraping by). People are pieces of a puzzle he's forever trying to solve, a quest that leads him to render their bodies and the way they live inside them, which are hardly ever the same thing. In life class, he could capture the model's resentment in a slash of charcoal down the page, so anyone looking at the drawing knew she didn't want to be there.

Looking at the faces at the table, he likes the play of shadow and light, but it's Rika's face he keeps coming back to. Ordinarily she's pale and plain (he's watched her off and on all week), but when something moves her, the face lights up and becomes nearly (not quite) beautiful. Her blue eyes widen, grow shiny and light. Blood rushes to the skin's surface. She lifts her head and smiles, bringing definition to the planes of her face, the broad forehead, wide cheekbones, and narrow jaw. She looks best when she's smiling; she smiles when he speaks to her, so she's the one he speaks to. As he watches the transformation, he likes knowing he's responsible. With the lamplight shining on her hair, her face pink with excitement, she's luminous, entirely different from last night, when her face looked drawn and sallow. Chin sunk on her fist, Rika listened while Jack went off on one of his boozy rants about the indignities of his life as a midlist novelist, and Ben watched her eyes glaze over.

Ben can't quite pinpoint the difference, but he knows that neither he nor Rika is quite at ease in this odd assortment of artists, writers, poets, and composers, all embarked on a common quest for space and solitude. He feels lucky to have not only a bedroom in the yellow farmhouse up the road but a light-filled studio overlooking the woods. Were he not here, he'd be hunched over drawings at the kitchen table in the apartment he shares with Mattie, a place not really big enough for two artists, their piles of materials and stacks of equipment, and then the work itself, rolled and stacked, flat-filed, hung, but little of it sold, not yet anyway. Sometimes, in that city apartment, in Chicago itself, he feels the onset of a slow suffocation.

What he loves about the Colony is the time to think, to walk the acres of hills and meadows and woods, to look at the oily slick of tadpoles swimming at the edge of the pond and not have to explain himself to anybody. Some days he speaks to no one until dinnertime. Some days, he's up at dawn; on others, he sleeps until noon. Sometimes he finds himself riveted by the sight of boulders scattered in the fields, by his fingers splayed against the trunk of a birch, by the smooth pale stalk of a woman's neck as she bends in sunlight to show him what she's found growing in the garden.

It is she who suggests the walk, she who smiles when Ben says that he'll come along, so why, then, does she turn to the others at the table and invite them as well? Rika asks herself this as she and Ben walk silently behind six or seven other residents, all laughing and talking together as they amble along the farm road. She tells herself she was only being polite, but small groups head out after dinner almost every evening, and it's understood that anyone who wishes to can join.

I'm afraid of being alone with Ben, she thinks, although it's also what she wishes for, to be alone in the deepening twilight with the young man who is telling her about geological formations in the upper Alleghenies, a place he knows because he spent his childhood here.

"Then how long have you lived in Chicago?" she asks.

"Three years," he says. "I only went there for graduate school." He snaps the head off a stalk of dry grass growing along the path. "I'm not wild about the city. I miss the woods."

Driving north a week ago, Rika enjoyed watching the season peel back, the lush green of North Carolina giving way to Virginia's bright acidic flush of new leaves, and finally the bare limbs and knotty, unopened buds of the trees that gray the Pennsylvania landscape. The sky is striated rose, palest near the treetops. Birches stand out against the solid mass of oaks and beeches as if someone chalked them in.

"These are your woods then," she says. "No wonder you seem so at home here."

All he says is, "Yup," and walks quietly through the darkening field, where barn swallows are swooping and diving, making a last meal of insects before dark.

She grew up only a couple of hours away, in Connecticut, but this is a secret she keeps from all but people she knows well. She especially doesn't advertise the fact to aspiring artists: Her mother is a well-known painter. Rika prefers her friends genuine.

When an owl hoots, she asks softly, "What kind of owl is that?"

Ben stops and listens. After a few minutes, he shakes his head and says, "I'd have to hear it again to be sure."

"Owls have such different calls," Rika says. "But I can never remember which is which. Barn or barred, I'm always mixing them up."

He looks down at her and smiles. "My dad was a birder. He used to take me along on walks. I grew up knowing what the birds sound like. The way somebody else might grow up knowing that the tree in their front yard's a maple."

"Some birds I recognize," Rika says, stooping to pick a piece of quartz off the path. She holds it up, a prize, then drops it into her skirt pocket. "But I can probably sing the theme song for every TV sit-com from the 1970s. That's the kind of childhood I had."

Ben gives her a long, speculative look, as if he sees through her self-deprecation. "You've taught yourself a lot, then," he says.

She feels suddenly shy. "I—well, my husband's also interested in nature," she says. "We walk in the woods when we can. We keep a garden. In the winter, we put up bird feeders." She hesitates, then adds, "Ethan reads a lot about nature. We both do."

When Ben doesn't respond, she shakes her head and says, "*Interested in nature.* God, that sounds stupid. Like you could be interested in nature the way someone might be interested in cars. Or golf."

"Yeah, I was just thinking that," Ben says.

She looks up at him, a little offended.

Then he says, "But I know what you mean. Nature's a big part of his life, so he takes the trouble to find out what things are called and why they do what they do. You both take the trouble. That's important."

"I think so," she says, realizing that not only has she dated herself by mentioning the 1970s, she's identified herself as part of a *we*. *What mire have you waded into, where every word takes on a new weight? You're trying too hard to make him like you,* she scolds herself, realizing that she hasn't felt this way around a man since—she bows her head, thinking—well, since she met Ethan, fourteen years ago.

The rest of the group have walked so far ahead, Rika feels almost like she and Ben are alone. She feels comfortable with him, as if they've known one another before, in a different lifetime. Looking sidelong at his face, she thinks tentatively, *You could touch me,* but seconds later she's surprised to realize, *I wouldn't mind if you kissed me.* The longer they walk in silence, the more she hopes he will. Maybe not immediately, but soon. Eventually.

He walks along with his hands in his coat pockets, almost as if he were entirely alone. Her hands tremble, and she doesn't quite know what to do with them, touching first her hair, then the collar of her jacket, then folding her arms across her chest.

"Are you cold?" he asks, and she says, "Of course not," then wonders *Why "of course not"? It's freezing out here.*

She hears the voices of the others waiting for them on the road, and as she and Ben draw nearer, their words come back to her in snatches, brief exclamations at the appearance of a star, something discovered in the bend of the path, a piece of wood or a bright stone.

A piece of wood, a star, a stone . . . begins the rhythm in her head, perhaps the first line of a poem. She repeats the words to herself a few times, trying to commit them to memory, but her head feels clouded, and the words don't stick.

She says, "I wonder . . ."

Ben looks down at her and smiles. "What?" he encourages.

She's not sure what she'd planned to say. *I wonder why I'm so taken with you?* He's not the best-looking man to ever pay attention to her, nor the cleverest. Finally, he seems rather ordinary, a nice-looking guy with a lot of growing up to do. But there's a familiarity about him that seems like kinship. And there's no mistaking the dizzying rush she feels just being near him. Meeting his eyes, she stammers, "Well . . . how do you start a painting?"

Still smiling, he shrugs. "I guess the same way you start a poem. Blind faith."

"I guess that's how most things start," she says.

Not smiling now, he meets her eyes. "Exactly," he says.

The group drifts apart as the residences come into view, the women turning off the path that leads to the blue cottage and Jack and the other men continuing up the road to the farmhouse. Surprised at her own boldness, Rika turns to Ben and asks if she can walk with him to get the book on Pennsylvania trees he's offered to lend her.

Sylvie, the grandmotherly sculptor who has the room across the hall from Rika, stops and looks back at them. "Why don't you just get it tomorrow?" she asks.

"Because I want to read it tonight," Rika says, trying to keep her voice light. For a moment, Sylvie seems to be trying to decide whether to join them, but then gives Rika a look, turns, and follows the other women into the cottage.

Rika takes a deep breath as she and Ben start toward his house. The other men are already out of sight, leaving the dark path empty. She can hardly believe she's done something so brazen, and feels herself trembling, not with cold. *This is where you take my hand*, she silently directs him, but Ben walks so briskly, Rika nearly has to trot to keep up with him, and he talks nonstop about the great weather they've had over the last couple of days. At the farmhouse door, he tells her he'll be right back, and leaves her standing in the vestibule beside the coatrack while he goes upstairs.

She looks around hoping Jack won't appear—he's been flirting with her all week, the geezer, and she wouldn't put it past him to waltz in and invite her to stay for a drink.

Ben reappears with the book a few minutes later, hands it to her without comment, and backs up until he's standing against the newel post, arms folded across his chest. She looks down at the floor, waiting, thanking him effusively in words she's not even conscious of forming. When her eyes meet his, she stops talking, and he asks if she needs a flashlight to guide her back down the hill. She takes the flashlight, then says that on second thought, she doesn't need it. "You can actually see better without a light," she says, and sounding a little irritated, he says, "I know that. But most people don't."

Rika waits for him to realize that he ought to at least offer to walk down the road with her, but after a brief silence, she says, "Well, if there's a bear, I guess I'll just scream."

Looking preoccupied, Ben nods.

"Good-night, then," she finally says, forcing herself to sound cheerful, and he closes the door behind her.

Back in her room, Rika's so cold she lies under her comforter with her jacket still on. She opens the book on trees but can't read more than a sentence or two before a searing thought comes into her head: how foolish she must've looked to Ben when he practically pushed her out the door. She can't imagine what he must think of her. She's not even sure what she thinks of herself.

How easy he could have made things if he'd only said what she wanted him to say: *Would you like some tea? A glass of wine? Want to see my new work?*

Any one of them, she thinks now, burrowing beneath the covers. *Any one of them would've given us more time . . . Instead, he pushed me out as if I were some slut.*

Sylvie's voice carries in the hallway, announcing that it shouldn't take an hour for Rika to walk up the hill to the other house and back. "Maybe we should send out a search party," another woman giggles, and Sylvie grumbles something Rika can't hear.

She lies there wondering if she should make an appearance, let the women know she's returned with her virtue intact. *People always think I'm so goddamned sweet and . . . tame*, she thinks, sitting up. *Let them be scandalized, I don't care.* But as they continue talking in low voices, she begins to feel a little tawdry. When she hears "a husband and child," to which Sylvie responds, "And besides, he's so young," she gets up, opens her door, and walks into the hall.

The two women look at her as if she's materialized out of thin air. "Hello," Rika says, walks past them into the bathroom, and shuts the door.

Splashing water over her face, Rika thinks, *You're pathetic, pathetic, pathetic.* In the next minute, scrutinizing herself in the mirror that hangs under the single unshaded bulb, she thinks, *The next move is definitely up to him.*

After little more than a week at the Colony, Ben's done so much work he's run short of fixative. He's headed to the art supply store in Summerville, easing down the dirt road in his truck, when he sees Rika sitting on the front porch of the cottage. He's just been thinking about her. On their quiet walk through the woods last night, he enjoyed being with someone—a woman—who knows that every species of owl has a different call, that there's a difference between a waxing and a waning moon. He's never read her poems, but he imagines they're like her pocketing of the rock on the road: a quick flash of observation, a lot of mystery.

He's never really known a poet, but that she is one makes him want to give her a lot of latitude. Anyone else, he'd be sure that walking back up to the house with him was a come-on. With Rika, it's entirely possible that she stayed up late reading about Pennsylvania forests. He likes that quality of frank curiosity she has about the natural world.

She's reading now, sitting on the porch in her *fairy clothes*, as he's heard Sylvie call them. While other women at the Colony seem to live in jeans, Rika's wrapped in complications of cotton and lace and thin wool, dyed rich shades of plum and indigo, viridian, ruby, cobalt, a smattering of earthy browns and blacks. So much cloth, it's easy to forget that a body's swaddled beneath it. Last night, she stumbled on the path and as he helped to right her, realized she didn't even reach his shoulder. Her feet are so small, her shoes look like children's shoes. But she's feisty; he can't imagine Mattie heading out alone into the rural night armed only with a copy of *Trees of Pennsylvania*. Rika didn't seem to blink an eye when she turned and headed out into the darkness.

Her feet are propped on the bottom rail of the banisters, and when he stops the truck and calls out "Good morning," she puts her feet down on the porch floor and calls back, "It's afternoon." He glances at his watch, sees she's right, and when he looks back she's picking her way across the front lawn, clutching a red notebook against her chest, hair falling around her shoulders, the first time he's seen it loose. With the light behind her, the colors are extraordinary—Venetian red against ultramarine, ultramarine against copper—and he smiles just seeing them pieced against the greening lawn, a collage of shapes united by hue. Her face barely reaches the window of his truck, which makes them both laugh. When she smiles, faint wrinkles fan around her eyes, which have a familiar warmth. How old is she? Thirty-five maybe?

Though he hadn't been planning to, he says, "Come into town with me?" and she says, "Give me five minutes," and almost runs back into the cottage.

When Rika comes down the steps she's put on a lumpy (possibly homemade?) cardigan, soft green, and a wide-brimmed, brown felt hat over her bright hair: She looks like a child playing dress-up. *What a tiny thing she is. Hardly to my shoulder.* The bones of her arm sharp beneath the soft cloth, something familiar in her eyes. He's smiling when he leans over and opens the door.

Rika can't remember the last time she was with someone capable of such silence. Ben drives this road far more slowly than she usually does, with both hands on the wheel, and occasionally a muscle twitches in his jaw, but he says nothing, just stares ahead out the windshield. Maybe he feels awkward about last night. She gnaws the inside of her bottom lip, deciding, *If he doesn't bring it up, I'm certainly not going to. The last thing I want is his pity.*

Rika looks around the truck's interior, playing a game with herself: What can she tell of his life from what she finds there? The compartment of dimes and quarters yields no secrets, but the open roll of peppermint Life Savers, silver earring, and tube of ChapStick in the cubby on the dash are more promising. In the map pocket of the passenger side door, there's a photography magazine, and she points to it and says, "And you're a photographer as well?"

He glances over and says, "That's Mattie's," taking his hand off the wheel long enough to open a bottle of water and drink from it. He says, "She's working on a BFA in photography at the Art Institute."

"Ah," she says, "your reason for staying in Chicago."

He nods. "She's finished in June. Then we're off to New York."

He's mentioned her before, of course, this Mattie, just as they've all mentioned partners back in the distant worlds they left to come here, as she herself has mentioned Ethan and her daughter Sara. Rika tries to recall what Ben said before she was paying much attention. Mattie's unhappy, perhaps, about him coming here? She thinks a month is too long to be apart? From this and other hints he's dropped, Rika surmises their relationship is not quite solidified. Still, they're planning to move to New York together.

Rika turns a little in her seat, facing him, trying to imagine him earnestly making plans with this unknown girl. Where do they have their serious talks? At the kitchen table? In bed? Which one of them asks, *How can we afford . . .* and which one says, *I think if we're careful, we can do this?* She feels an unexpected pang, thinking of Mattie, probable owner of the silver earring and a reader of *F-Stop*, an undergraduate, no doubt beautiful and brilliant.

She's twenty-two, tops, Rika thinks. Mattie: The name alone conjures someone determined and capable, with unflappable poise. Perky. She ran track in high school, Rika realizes. And played piano. And she always tans instead of burns.

Rika asks, "What kind of work does she do?" and when Ben frowns and says, "Sorry?" she says, "This Mattie. Her photographs. What are they like?"

He sets the water bottle back in the cup holder, looks out the windshield, and shrugs. "Rocks, mostly," he offers. "She likes to go out with her camera and just . . . find an interesting place and start shooting. For her thesis, she's doing a series on erratics that's pretty great." He glances over at Rika, then looks back at the road. "I think you'd like them," he says.

How would you know? Rika thinks, unsure if he means this as a compliment: *You have something in common with the woman I love.* She studies his profile, backlit by the side window. His skin is finely grained as the skin on the inside of her wrist, smooth ivory, poreless. *Grown men don't have skin that flawless. And I've never seen such deep blue eyes. Is he really vain enough to wear colored contacts?*

She rescinds her judgment of him as ordinary: *He's absolutely beautiful.* But as she watches him obliquely, keeping her face turned slightly to the windshield, she sees that age is already making its mark. Austerity's begun to overlay the childhood sweetness. A vague tightness around the mouth, a subtle narrowing of the eyes: Something ungenerous in him, she thinks, remembering his quick frown, the flashes of impatience, his cutting dismissals of other artists. And the silences: Perhaps she's been wrong to think of them as peaceful, a sign of self-containment.

Silence can mean anything, she thinks, leaning back against the seat. After a moment, she says, "Has she ever photographed you?"

"Oh sure," he says, and smiles thinly, a touch of irony in his voice. "I'm her default subject. Always around."

Though she asked the question intending to follow it up with a question about the difference between being the artist and the subject, despite herself, what immediately comes to Rika's mind are Stieglitz's photographs of O'Keeffe, the documenting of a passion by recording the body of the beloved in minute detail. Is it the same, she wonders, a man's body seen through a woman's eyes? Does the arching of his ribcage, the dip of his pelvis, the smooth skin of his back become testament to the delight his body gives her? Can the hollow behind his knee become an expression of tenderness, or the sinews of his arms depict tension between them? What must his lover make of the notch of his clavicle, exposed now above the open collar of his shirt? Like an indentation made by a thumb.

Rika looks up at his face. "Do you mind being photographed?" she asks.

He takes the cap off his water bottle, wipes the mouth of it on his shirtsleeve, and hands it to her before saying, "Good question." When she sits holding the bottle without drinking, he gives her a wry smile and says, "I don't—you know—have anything."

"Ah," Rika says. "Sorry, still thinking about the photographs." She drinks, then holds the bottle out to him but he waves it away.

"Keep it," he says. "We're almost there."

When he says nothing more after a minute or so, Rika says, "So why is it a good question?"

He glances at her, brow furrowed. "Oh, right," he says. He wipes the back of his hand carefully against his lower eyelid, and she thinks, *He is wearing contacts.* He says, "I'm happy to give her something to photograph. If I'm working and she's taking pictures, it doesn't bother me. I don't much like to pose." They've come to the outskirts of the small town, and as he downshifts, he says. "Let me rephrase that. I don't pose. But sometimes when I look at the photos she's taken, I understand why some people think the camera steals the soul."

Rika studies him for a moment. "You mean it begins to seem like a violation?"

"Yeah, absolutely," he says. "I want to take that part of myself back. The part I didn't know she was getting. How did she see that? I wonder." He hesitates before saying, "Not that this would wash with Mattie, the part about taking myself back. She's tenacious." He gives Rika a brief grin of collusion, which she returns—almost gratefully, she notices.

To save time in town, they split up, Rika off to browse the boutiques, and Ben straight to the art supply store, where everything's overpriced. He's annoyed with himself for not packing the full can of fixative, for taking the one that was nearly empty. *I can always use more fixative,* he thinks, offering himself the usual consolation for an unexpected expense. *It's only the second week—I'll do a lot more work before the month's over.*

In addition to the fixative, he finds a jar of powdered smalt, a blue pigment ("beautiful, but unfortunately carcinogenic," say the books) that he hasn't been able to find in his usual haunts, and several sheets of cold-press, handmade paper that the clerk sells for half-price after Ben tells her he's at the Colony; she even throws in a few drawing pencils without charge ("You wouldn't believe the mark-up on these," she says, smiling).

He's coming out of the store with the rolled paper in one hand and a plastic bag in the other when he spots Rika walking into a shop on the opposite side of the street. He hesitates, thinking he'll just meet her at the diner for lunch as they'd planned, but then remembers how slow Mattie can be in stores like these, and he really wants to work this afternoon.

"Those are nice," he says, coming up behind Rika just as she lifts a pair of dangling amber earrings from the display.

She turns and smiles. "I was about to try them on."

He watches her push the thin, gold wires through the holes in her earlobes. The sales clerk—a skinny little blond—comes up and asks if they need help.

"I think I might want these," Rika says. "Ben, what do you think?"

He's about to say that it doesn't matter what he thinks, but the look of expectation on her face stops him. "Well, I can't tell anything with that hat on," he says, and she takes it off, allowing her hair to fall around her shoulders. The stones are the same dark honey color as her hair, a fact he remarks on.

"But do you like them?" Rika says, holding her hair back with one hand and turning her face from side to side.

He hesitates. Something in this gesture distracts him. "Yeah," he finally says. "I guess so."

Rika turns to the clerk and tells her she'll take the earrings, that she'll wear them home.

The clerk gives him a coy smile after she's rung up the sale. "If her man likes it, a woman has to buy it," she says, and Ben watches a blush splotch Rika's neck and creep up into her face as she signs the credit-card receipt.

Out on the sidewalk, he keeps expecting Rika to laugh and say something ironic, something like, "Well, that was weird."

Ella's Diner is famous for its lunches. At least, that's what Ben says. They're sitting at a table in a window alcove, Rika with her back to the street and Ben facing the window. As they wait for their order, Rika says, "When were you last here?"

Ben says, "Years ago. A friend from college has a vacation house in the Poconos. Sometimes on breaks, we'd come up here."

She tilts her head down and smiles, looking up at him. "An old girlfriend?"

He leans forward, resting his forearms against the edge of the table, and gives her a searching look. "Why do you ask?" His voice is low, his eyes unwavering.

Rika makes herself hold his gaze. With the light striking him this way, his hair's the color of bleached grass. Even his eyelashes are blond. Though it's cool in the diner, sweat prickles beneath her arms, her palms are damp, and she knows she's blushing. He looks at her as if he's trying to solve a problem—which color she might be, which line would best delineate her. Why did she ask? She can't even remember what they were talking about. To stop herself from touching his face, from putting her hand over his, from reaching out to push the blond curls away from his forehead, she clasps her hands before her on the table. "I'm just teasing," she says.

Raising his eyebrows, Ben draws a deep breath and looks away. Rika picks up her glass and takes a long drink of water. As she's about to set it down, the glass slips in her hand. She doesn't drop it, but water splashes across the tabletop. Before she can react, Ben's already grabbed a handful of napkins from the chrome dispenser.

"Don't worry," he soothes as she stammers an apology. "We're all right. Nothing's broken here."

Back in the truck, Rika's busy twisting her hair into a bun and securing it with pins, when Ben turns to her and says, "So, what's your husband do?"

She takes the last hairpin out of her mouth and pushes it into the thick mass at her nape before she speaks. "Owns a bookstore," she says.

Ben nods, and when she doesn't say anything else, he says, "You guys have been together a long time?"

"You guys," she says. "You make us sound like a rock band. Or a baseball team." Finally, she says, "Fourteen years."

Rika can practically see him doing the calculations in his head. "I'm thirty-four," she says. "If that's what you're asking." She folds her arms and looks out the side window, at the trees whipping past. She bites the inside of her lower lip to keep herself from saying more, because she's on the verge of blurting that she can't figure out why being close to him this way makes her feel almost sick with desire. *I don't play around*, she silently tells him. *I love my husband . . . really.*

Instead, after a few minutes of silence, she turns to him and says, "So, tell me about this smalt. What's it made from?" She takes the small bottle from the bag on the seat between them and holds it up to the light. Smalt: such a pure, clear blue, she'd believe him if he said it was made from powdered sky. "A color this beautiful should have a better name," she says. "*Smalt* sounds ugly."

He seems not to hear her. Staring thoughtfully out the windshield, he says, "When I moved in with Mattie, I decided if we were going to live together, we were going to be together, you know?"

Don't, she thinks, pulling her green sweater closer around her. If she could disappear inside it, she would. *Don't explain why you're not interested in me*, she silently begs him. *Please*. Rika returns the bottle of pigment to the bag.

"Right," she says.

"Mattie knows how I feel," Ben says. "But still, if I get a phone call, she wants to know who it is. If I'm late coming home, she wants to know where I've been. On the weekends, which is the only real time I have to do my work, she gets pissed because I won't go out dancing with her."

"It's not easy being married to an artist," Rika says. With an artist for a mother, she knows too well how difficult they can be to live with.

Ben glances over at her. "We're not married," he says. "Though I guess we might as well be. Before I came up here, we had a huge fight. I told her, 'Look, I'm going there to do my work, not to screw around,' but still, she wants me to phone her every night. She wants the play-by-play of what I've done since the last time I talked to her."

Rika clicks her tongue against the roof of her mouth. "She's afraid she'll lose you," she says, straightening up in the seat. She turns to look at him, this man the young woman back in Chicago loves. "You're really nice-looking," she says. "You're intelligent, sensitive. And you're very . . ." she shrugs, unsure of the word she should use, "approachable. She knows it wouldn't be difficult for a woman to become taken with you."

The muscle in his jaw twitches. "I'm not naïve," he says. He looks at her again and his voice trembles a little when he says, "I'm not a kid, though you probably think so."

"I don't, actually." For a moment, heart pounding, Rika thinks he may be working up to making a pass. Then as she watches his face, she realizes he's just stating a fact: At lunch he told her he was twenty-seven, and twenty-seven is not a kid. By the time she was twenty-seven, she'd been married six years and had a five-year-old daughter. In most ways, she feels younger now than she did then.

"Can I ask you something?" Ben says, glancing over at her.

Rika's palms are damp. She pushes a few stray wisps of hair behind her ears. "Of course."

"Does your husband act like that?" Ben says. "On your case about how you spend your time?"

"Ethan?" she says, a sudden heaviness in her belly at realizing that Ben sees her as a dispenser of sisterly advice, but some relief in it too. "Good Lord, no."

Ben says, "How'd he feel about your coming up here? A month's a long time to be away from home."

"He and Sara are fine without me. His mother comes up and takes charge. Everybody has a great time," Rika says, then looks at him evenly. "Besides, he trusts me."

"Well, that's important," Ben says, making the turn onto the state road back to the Colony. "Maybe the most important thing of all."

After a few miles, she says, "Would you please shift into third? The engine's lugging."

"Lugging?" he says. "What's lugging?"

She makes an engine sound in her throat, surprisingly accurate, and they both laugh.

"Are you always this bossy?" Ben asks her, and smiling, she says, "Yes."

That night, standing at the window of his room in the dark, he tells Mattie about the drive to Summerville.

"A poet?" she says doubtfully. "What's she like?"

"Nice," he says. "About forty. Sort of plain. She's married, with kids."

The laughter of relief: "Well, I was wondering." Mattie, who is beautiful in any light, smiles, and he hears it in her voice. "God, I miss you so much," she says.

"Everyone here is old," he reassures her, staring out at the shapes of trees against a moonless sky. "It's like being trapped at one of my parents' parties."

"Did your parents have parties?" she asks.

"Well, no. It's just a figure of speech."

"Trapped at a party," she muses. "Well . . . that couldn't be too bad."

Lying on her hard white bed in the hour before dinner, the warm afternoon sun streaking in, Rika opens her red notebook and writes on the first blank page:

> *Remind me why you didn't want another child.*
> *Remind me what you saw in me. Remind me*
> *Why you cut down the silver maple*
> *I always said I loved. And the pink rose*
> *Beneath the bedroom window—that went too,*
> *In the blight of your unforgiving.*

What disaster is she anticipating? No one has cut down the silver maple. The pink rose perished of rose sickness, long ago. And she agreed, didn't she, that one child was best, given the lives she and Ethan were trying to lead? Why does the thought of her clamped-off fallopian tubes make her feel desiccated, like a dead insect or a husk, like she's dead inside?

Rika sits up on her bed, tapping her pen on her knee. She remembers, not so many years ago, standing at her bedroom window, looking down at her wildered garden, wondering if a two-story fall would kill her. "Probably not," she murmured, and Ethan, coming up behind and enfolding her in his arms, said, "Probably not what?"

Ethan and Sara are her family. Ethan knows her better than anyone, this patient, intelligent man to whom women still give second looks on the street. And despite her glooms and moodiness, her sharp tongue, the days when she barely speaks, he remains kind. If she had to account to him for her feelings for Ben, she's afraid all she could say is, *It has nothing to do with you.*

She feels ashamed of herself for falling back on a phrase she never understood until now. She imagines Ethan pressing her to explain her desire. *This doesn't make sense*, she can almost hear him say. She feels his bewilderment that she could love someone else. She can see the look of disappointment on his face when she murmurs, *I can't explain, I just know how I feel.*

She fears his disappointment: with her, her inconstancy, her infidelity. *Don't you think I've been tempted, Rika? But we're married. I love you. We're raising a child together. We're a family.*

With absolute incredulity: That's how he'd respond.

Leaning back against the pillow, she hugs her elbows against her chest and stares through her open curtains out to the road.

For all I know, Ben has about as much interest in me as I have in Jack, she scolds herself. And has a brief, horrifying thought: Ben on the phone with Mattie, laughing about the married woman who's made him the object of her foolish romance. Her stomach knots; she tears the poem out of her notebook and crumples it.

She begins a straightforward chronicle of her days, counting them out, fourteen since she left North Carolina, seven since her discovery of the peony shoots, six since the trip to Summerville. She resolves never to write of Ben. When she gets home, Ethan can read her journal, as she sometimes suspects he does, and find that she's been as steadfast and sensible as ever.

And so she doesn't mention that she and Ben sit beside each other every evening at the table, or that, tramping the woods and meadows, they almost always walk side-by-side. She doesn't write that she looks forward to this time all day.

She doesn't write about plucking a leaf from Ben's hair and feeling the brief sensation under her fingers of springy coarseness, so unlike her own fine, silky hair, and Ethan's, and Sara's.

Instead, she lists the names of the trees she's seen, the birds she's spotted or heard calling, most of them identified by Ben. *Every night after dinner, we go walking in the woods, and sometimes an owl hoots,* she writes. *The peonies are little plants now, not fingers anymore.*

One morning in the third week of the residency, while Ben's eating breakfast, Jack stumbles into the kitchen. After fumbling around in the refrigerator for a while, he turns to Ben and says, "You know, I'm a little surprised you're the one she ended up with."

Ben looks up at him. "Excuse me?" he says.

Jack waves his hand dismissively. "Don't play the innocent," he says. He pours himself a cup from the pot of coffee Ben's just brewed and leans back against the counter. "For a couple days, I thought I might have a chance," he says. "But I guess you're smoother than you look." Jack laughs, a harsh sound in the quiet room. He sighs and scratches his chest.

Ben refills his bowl with Cheerios as he contemplates what to say. He chews a few mouthfuls of cereal before deciding that he might as well say nothing. He looks at Jack, shrugs and continues eating.

"How old is Rika anyway?" Jack asks. "Thirty-five?" He waits. "Forty?"

"I don't know," Ben says.

"That's splitting hairs at this point, huh?" Jack whistles through his teeth for a few seconds. "What are you, twenty-three, twenty-four?"

"Somewhere in there," Ben says.

Jack says, "The woman I'm married to now was one of my students. I'm practically old enough to be her grandfather. She's crazy about me."

"Lucky for you," Ben says.

Head tilted, frowning, Jack studies the coffee in his cup. "It's weird, though. When the woman's older, it's . . ." he wiggles his fingers in the air, "a little too kinky or something."

Ben puts down his spoon. "You know, Jack . . ." he starts.

"I'm almost seventy," Jack says. "And if I think about making it with a ninety-year old broad, my dick shrivels up to my ears.. But somebody fifty? Bring her on. And somebody thirty? Believe me, I still get offers."

Elbow resting on the table, Ben cups his chin in his palm. He looks down at the wood tabletop, scarred with cup rings and cigarette burns.

"It's a little unusual, is all I'm saying," Jack says. "But if you like it, why the hell not, right?"

Ben nods slightly, still looking at the table. "Thanks, Jack."

"She might teach you a few things," Jack says. He pauses. "Or vice-versa. God knows, looking at her, it's hard to tell."

"Do me a favor," Ben says. "Don't worry about it."

Jack sighs. "Yeah, yeah, yeah," he says. "You already know everything. I thought I did too, at your age." On his way out of the kitchen, he pats Ben on the shoulder and says, "You just . . . be careful, okay?"

Finishing his coffee, Ben thinks about what it must mean, *to be careful*. He's never much cared what other people think, but lately, he, too, is a little worried about Rika. She's funny and smart and attentive. And she talks to him about his work, which no one else here really does. In fact, his work is mostly what they talk about; it's only later, back in his room, that he realizes he hasn't asked about hers. For the first time, he has a woman for a friend, without all the complications of desire . . . although sometimes just a look she gives him, or something she says, makes him wonder how uncomplicated things between them really are. A few times, he's been pretty sure that all he'd have to do is touch her, and they'd be lovers. But in the next instant, her demeanor's changed, and she's an older sister again, a translator of the world's peculiarities. He's pretty sure that, given time, they could become good friends. As their stay at the Colony dwindles, though, he's beginning to suspect that of everyone he's met, Rika's the one he can't bring back into his real life.

What would Mattie think about her? He can't even begin to imagine. But that's not the only reason. There's a heaviness in the air when he's with Rika—everything feels loaded, meaningful in a way that he's starting to find oppressive. Years of history seem bound up between them, though he barely knows her.

Time to detach, he tells himself. He's good at aloofness. He's had a lot of practice in it.

When Rika comes out to the cottage porch, Sylvie's already there, smoking a cigarette. Tall, silver-haired, elegant, Sylvie works mostly in stone. Often, she comes to dinner with a respirator hanging around her neck and her clothes caked in dust, but this evening she has on clean jeans, a sleek, black sweater.

"Going to dinner? I'll walk with you," she tells Rika and grinds her cigarette out on the porch before carefully dropping it into the / Ziploc bag she carries in her purse. "It's my nasty habit," she says. "Others shouldn't be subjected to it."

When they're a little way down the gravel path to the road, Sylvie says, "So, Ben's showing his work tonight." She speaks as if this is something Rika already knows.

Rika says, "Yes," trying not to sound surprised. She hasn't seen much of Ben over the last few days; he's excused himself from the after-dinner walks by saying he's trying to finish some paintings before their time at the Colony ends, just a few days from now.

Sylvie puts an arm around Rika's shoulder. "Ben's such a darling," she says, and gives her a squeeze. "He's exactly the kind of man I wish my daughter would date. Sensitive. Intelligent. So good-looking. He'll make a great father someday."

Then she says, "The other night, I was watching the two of you together, and I had an amazing revelation."

Rika's mouth is dry. Sylvie says, "When I see him with you, being so considerate, looking out for you the way he does, it's just so sweet, so unusual in a person his age. And I know he must really, really love his mother. I love that about him. Don't you?"

Ben kicks the metal legs out from beneath the folding work table and leans it against the wall. What was it Mattie said on the phone last night when he grumbled about people coming into the studio? *Don't complain, maybe somebody will buy something.* Even so, it's an interruption, this quaint ritual of opening one's studio to the other artists at the Colony. Why he's volunteered to go first, he's not sure—perhaps just to be done with it. He dreads their comments on his work—the inevitable off-base comparisons and forced analogies. Truth to tell, he's not too interested in what anyone has to say about his paintings; he has enough opinions of his own.

And then, of course, there's Rika. Aside from friendly, neutral conversations at the dinner table, he's successfully avoided her for a few days. When he declines to join the group for the ritual walk afterward, the look of disappointment that crosses her face is almost enough to make him change his mind, and he understands that guilt is an inevitable part of this relationship. *I've done nothing, aside from being sociable*, he reminds himself. *It's her problem if she feels hurt. I haven't encouraged her.*

"Oh, lighten up," Mattie's told him. "She has a crush on you. That's all. I think it's kind of cute."

But it's not that at all, not a *crush*, he thinks as he straightens one of his paintings. Lots of women—and men, too—have had crushes on him. This is different—nothing in Rika's manner toward him is light or giddy. She wants something from him, he feels it—something complicated; she's not just fooling around.

He stands back against the doorjamb and looks critically at his paintings. Not a bad month's work, although the longer he stands there examining the paintings hung together, the less certain of them he feels. *What the fuck am I doing?* he asks himself, running his hand down his face and then over the back of his neck. These paintings are nothing like his usual work. All he's done is record what he's seen around him. There's no spark, no imagination in any of it. How will he even make use of this when he gets back home? A month wasted is what this has been—a month of landscape painting for someone who doesn't paint landscapes. A waste of everyone's fucking time.

What he would like most to do right now is get in his truck and drive away, who knows where, come back tomorrow, maybe, just long enough to pack. *Well, what's stopping you, buddy?*

He glances at his watch. He's missed dinner altogether. But he couldn't eat anyway: His stomach is in knots. Although he should be used to it after the grueling crits in graduate school, showing his work always fries his nerves.

They all crowd into Ben's studio in the woods, Rika at the very back, beside the door. While the others comment, Ben looks on, nodding or shaking his head, occasionally interrupting to ask a question. Arms folded across his chest, he doesn't even glance at Rika, which makes the pull she feels toward him all the stronger.

She tries to remember their last conversation, worries (*like a schoolgirl*, she thinks, *this is ridiculous*) that she said something stupid. She gnaws on her bottom lip and shifts her weight to the other foot as she wishes everyone would just clear out and leave them alone to talk. In a few days he'll be gone from her life forever, maybe without even knowing how she feels. Would anything change if he did know?

Rika feels something important—life-changing, perhaps—slipping from her grasp.

While she waits, she looks at his paintings. They're stylistically similar to his drawings—the landscapes and architectural studies he's been doing around the Colony are marvels of small detail. The paintings have the same tightness and precision, a nearly photographic accuracy that disappoints her. She's long regarded photorealism as—to use her mother's term—just *dick-wagging. See what I can do?* To paint a forest dappled with sunlight and make it look like a photograph of a forest dappled with sunlight—well, what's the point? And yet here are paintings of the woods around the Colony dappled with sunlight. Rika squints, hoping she's missing something.

As the others leave, Rika draws nearer, arms hugging her chest. When she finally looks away from the wall of canvases, everyone else has gone, and Ben's standing near, arms folded across his chest, staring at the paintings.

"This isn't what I was expecting," she says, unable to keep disappointment from her voice.

Ben glances at her, then back at the wall of paintings. "No?" he says, wiping the corner of one eye with his index finger. His face is so dispassionate, the paintings might belong to someone else.

Rika waits, but he doesn't ask her what she means. It occurs to her that he might not care. After a moment, he leans over and scrapes at something on one canvas with his thumbnail.

Rika says, "I didn't expect them to be so realistic."

He smirks. "You thought I was more *creative* than that," he says.

"You say *creative* like it's a dirty word."

He says, "When you talk about your poems, you say that the most important thing to you is accuracy."

"Yes."

"So how is this different? These paintings are accurate. You have to admit. If nothing else, they're accurate."

This isn't the conversation Rika wants to be having, standing here alone with Ben in his studio, the door and windows open to the night. He stares her down. She hesitates before she says, "There's a difference between recording something as it is and making art out of it."

"Wow," he says. "Zing."

"When I look at these paintings," she goes on, "I think yes, they're exquisitely crafted, but they're a little short on emotional truth."

"*Emotional truth?* What's that?"

Rika gives him a searching look. She's not sure if he's being sarcastic. "Where are you in any of them?"

He leans in and puts his forefinger square on a patch of meticulously executed woods. "Right here," he says.

He's hurt, she thinks. *Something's wrong with him.*

Bad wrong.

Although she can't name what the something is, she feels she's found the key to a strange map she has, until now, been trying to read unaided. For all his seeming confidence, his pedigree, his bravado, he doesn't have a clue. He's making it up as he goes along, just as she is.

She'd like to acknowledge this, allow him to see that it's what they're all doing, really, that it doesn't matter if what's here now is half-baked or badly thought out.

"It's just a matter of selection," she says, and when she puts her hand over his hand touching the canvas, she could be comforting her daughter, she feels that tender toward him, that empty of desire.

He jerks his hand away as if she's burned him. "Look," he says, "you'd better go."

She smiles and shakes her head slightly.

"Hey, I didn't mean . . ."

The look he turns on her silences her immediately. She takes a step back. His eyes, cold and sharp, accuse her of what she has only allowed herself to think, tell her he knows what she is under the veneer of sweetness and compassion: predatory, unfaithful, someone who doesn't deserve to be trusted.

"No?" he says.

She squares her shoulders. "No," she says.

As he says nothing more, just stands looking at her with an expression of profound skepticism, she turns and leaves the studio.

On the dark path back to the blue cottage, she begins to think of other things she might have said.

"Save it," she mutters to herself. "Save it for the poems."

Erratics

Erratic #112

At a crowded loft party in Williamsburg, on a hot September night, if any breeze came through the open windows, it was gone by the time it reached him; his throat felt as if he'd been huffing dust. A waiter passed with a black-lacquered tray held above shoulder-height, on it several tall, sweaty glasses of what looked like iced-water. When they made eye contact, Ben signaled, but he walked on. Ben followed, but the waiter stayed ahead, making his way through the crowd with the tray balanced on his open palm. People parted to let him through, and had to part again when Ben approached, but this time—Ben was just a man, not a waiter doing his job—they moved reluctantly, as if he were an intruder.

Newly arrived from Chicago, where he and Mattie had gone to art school, Ben knew almost no one at the party. Before they'd even gotten their drinks, Mattie wandered off to talk with the guy who'd invited her, whose loft they were seeing for the first time. Ben lost sight of her, and now kept his eye on the tray of glasses bobbing through the crowd. Occasionally, someone stopped the waiter and removed a glass from the tray. Ben was afraid by the time he reached him, the drinks would all be gone.

As he made his way through the room, his thirst seemed to grow exponentially. The glasses looked so cool. He had no trouble imagining how delicious the water—if that's what it was—would taste. He knew exactly how the sweating glass would feel in his hand.

He'd have called out to the waiter, if calling would have done any good. He kept following until the man disappeared through a door.

When Ben looked around, he was near a table where two other waiters were pouring wine and opening bottles of beer. He grabbed a bottle of Molson's and downed it, gratefully, then asked for another. But the beer didn't quench his thirst.

Mattie came over with their host, who wanted to meet him, and as they talked, he had another beer, and gradually he forgot about the cold glasses on the tray, stopped thinking about how good the water would have tasted.

Erratic #35

Ben's father, Henry Tillman, the well-known children's book writer and illustrator, died on January third. Henry's wife Kerry phoned from Pennsylvania at five o'clock on a freezing Chicago morning, still sitting beside Henry's body on the daybed in his studio, waiting for the undertaker to arrive. Beside Ben in their bed, Mattie stirred, pushed her hair out of her eyes, and watched him talk to a woman he knew from the handful of times he'd visited his father over the four years she and Henry had been together.

Ben's glad he can remember Mattie that way, soft and full of sleep, her hand on his chest gentle and her words, when he got off the phone, kind. It's like a photograph, which seems appropriate because that's what Mattie does: takes photographs.

But a photograph implies a single truth, a clarity. The shutter closes down on a moment in time. The resulting image is what was before you.

Erratic #7

Here is Mattie, lying on her belly in the parking lot of their apartment building a few weeks after they arrived in Brooklyn, fiddling with a tabletop tripod. On a small hill of bare dirt between the macadam and the fence, she's placed a smooth, white rock the size of her palm. Against the fence she's thumbtacked an enlarged photograph of a prairie sky mackereled with clouds. She takes a photograph of the rock on the hill of bare dirt, with the photograph of the sky out of focus behind it. She calls it "Erratic #7" and a couple years later will include it in a show of her photographs of boulders left behind by the last glaciers. Some of the boulders are as large as the cars that were parked in the lot where she took the photograph of the rock.

Erratic #28

Ben fights his mind's impulse to jump away from Mattie before he can think of more. He wants to let this single episode—this sleight-of-hand, this deceit—stand for their shared life, though it's only emblematic of the end, when perception, scale, and authenticity became difficult to parse. Because it happens last, he likes to believe that the ending contains an entire history he'd have noticed sooner if he'd known what to look for.

But to focus only on the ending eliminates the surface appeal that drew him and Mattie together. It relieves him of the responsibility of remembering the rain as they walked to her apartment the night they first made love. It erases the mornings he watched her sleeping. The tenderness she showed—baking a cake on his birthday, rubbing his back, cutting his hair, renting a movie she thought he might like—is gone in a cloud of dust. The unstable core that withstands neither sudden shifts nor unusual pressure was forged from their bodies.

So what if all they found at the center was ash? How did they even know it was the center, not just an insulating ring around the fire?

Erratic #83

Whatever he thinks about Mattie is shadowed by what those thoughts reveal about him. When Mattie smiled, her whole face lit up, so she didn't smile often. She fought against her natural sweetness, fearing it might make her sentimental. Although it was Jane Austen that she loved and read, she referenced Heidegger in all her artist statements because she thought this sounded smarter. When people asked about her background, she slanted details toward rough-hewn working class, omitting that in New Orleans there stands a canary-colored clapboard shop scrolled in gingerbread where her parents sell birdhouses painted fulsome hues and trays decoupaged with red snakes, blue dogs, and alligators.

Erratic #45

Mattie will not bear children. Through the miracle of genetic testing, Mattie knows she's a carrier of the disease that runs through the women of her family. Any male she gives birth to has a fifty-percent chance of inheriting the disease; any female has the same chance of being a carrier.

I'm sorry, she said the day she told Ben that if he wanted a family, he'd better bark up another tree.

She said it just that way, *bark up another tree*, without remorse or inflection, and he looked at her and wondered why she was so furious at him. All he had said was, "If we ever have kids, I hope . . ."

This isn't my fault, he started to say, but then she turned and walked out of the apartment and didn't come home until long past dark.

Erratic #62

What Ben knows for sure is that the color of Mattie's hair and eyes is irrelevant. They were given to her before she had any say in the matter, handed down through generations of salt and sweat and religious fervor. Better to remember the smell of her breath or the row of brown freckles splayed across the creamy skin of her inner thigh. He used to trace those stars as if they were on a map of the sky. He wanted to think if he steered by them, he'd always find the right way home, but not even he believed this. They were just concentrations of pigment under the skin.

Mattie is not a fixed point in time. Mattie is not still shedding her light from the same place in the universe. He's not still gazing up at the constellations from his own dark place in the field.

Among the chilly women of Chicago, she alone took him in her arms. Her clean, open face might have sparked a hundred imaginations, but in that iced-over park beside the river, it was his imagination she fired. And he was grateful. Who knows? Had they stayed in Chicago, they might be together still.

Erratic #74

Mattie left her husband to get to Chicago, walked out of their well-appointed condo with nothing more than her clothes and her cameras, and never looked back. She'd been in the B.F.A. photo program for three years when Ben arrived to do an M.F.A. in painting. Since she's a few years older than he is, Ben thought she was a graduate student or maybe even adjunct faculty when he met her at a party his first semester.

"Nope," she said, taking a swig of her beer and crinkling her eyes at him in a way that he came to understand was Mattie's version of flirting. "I'm just so poor, it's taking me twice as long."

She said she supported herself by winning scholarships and taking photographs of the blessed moments of people's lives.

"I swear to God," she said, putting her hand over her heart. "I have even taken pet photos. I have no shame." She crinkled her eyes at him again. "Do you have a pet?"

When he said he didn't, she said, "That's too bad. I have two cats. You can meet them if you'd like."

"Sure," he said.

"Come for dinner tomorrow night then," she said.

Months later, after he'd moved in with her, she said, "I can't believe how I steamrolled you that first night. I've never acted that way in my life."

"You were a little drunk," he said.

"I was cold sober," she said. "The beer was simply a prop to disarm you."

He nudged her hair back and kissed behind her ear. "Making you seem approachable," he said.

"And then . . ." she laughed and closed her arms around him. "Gotcha."

Erratic #11

Back then Ben painted teenaged boys. Something about the physical awkwardness that they tried to hide behind bravado, even their pimply faces and lank hair, intrigued him. He'd completed about twenty large paintings of these juvenile hipsters, all meticulously executed in oils, meticulously copied from pencil drawings that he had, in turn, meticulously copied from photographs he downloaded from the social-networking pages of strangers. The work won him admission to grad school, but soon after enrolling at the Art Institute, he began to suspect he didn't really like to paint. Everything about the medium—the mess, the smell, the cumbersome equipment, the space the finished paintings took up—everything began to irritate the hell out of him.

Though his professors talked to the students a lot about pushing beyond their self-imposed boundaries, Ben got the best response from them when he painted the boys; he soon embraced the idea that he had an obsession. Since at least one self-portrait appeared in each painting, this vein he was mining was termed self-discovery, something to be "worked through," like a series of caves. By his second year, he was feeling more like he'd reached a dead-end in the dark.

Erratic #26

"You seem bored," Mattie remarked one morning as she stood in his studio watching him work, a cup of coffee in her hand. "You shouldn't paint if you don't want to paint."

He wiped his hands on a rag and looked over at her. "I'll lose my fellowship if I don't paint," he said.

"Let's take a walk," she said. "When we come back, you'll feel more like painting."

"Give me a sip of your coffee?" He looked out the window. "It's snowing."

"So?" She handed the cup over.

"I think I'm getting sick. Maybe the paint's making me sick. Or the solvents."

"It happens," Mattie said. "Photographers get cancer all the time from the chemicals."

"Cheery thought," he said. "Doesn't that worry you?"

Mattie shrugged. "I'd rather get it from photo chemicals than from breathing car exhaust or factory spume," she said. "I'm careful. Besides, now there's digital. At least I have a choice."

He handed the cup back, but she waved it away. "Finish it," she said and turned to go. "Call me if you want to go for a walk. I'll be in the lab, printing."

Even as Ben won prizes and became the new star in the painting program, the hours spent dabbing paint on a canvas or wood panel seemed to him, finally, a stupid way to spend one's life.

"Everybody goes through this," Mattie said one night as she scanned negatives into the computer. "You'll work your way into something new."

Erratic #64

He got his M.F.A. after two years and went to work at Whole Foods while Mattie made a push to finish her degree. Working gave him a head start on knowing how it felt to be out of school, with no real community and no one clamoring to see the painting he'd just finished. He never had to paint again, if he didn't want to. But he knew plenty of people who used to paint, including half the people he worked with, and pride kept him from numbering himself among the crowd.

"Why don't you just draw?" Mattie said. "You like to draw. Don't worry about painting for a while."

Mattie had her own stress. She'd borrowed money from her ex-husband to go to school full-time for a final year. Most nights when Ben went to bed at eleven, she was still up, and sometimes she was still up at five, when he got up to get ready for work.

When he came home at two in the afternoon, Mattie was gone to class. He showered, made a pot of coffee, and tried to paint. He didn't know what else to do.

Erratic #19

Always before, when Ben had a problem with his work, he had his father to talk to, but now when he phoned, Henry barely seemed interested. One night he said, "Ben, there comes a point where you just have to figure it out on your own. Nobody can tell you what you need to be doing."

Ben felt stung. Henry had said similar things to him over the years, but this time, the words seemed a dismissal. *It's not my problem anymore*, he might have been saying, *I have more important things to think about.*

Ben emailed him photos of the new paintings but didn't hear back. "He must think they're pretty bad," Ben told Mattie.

She squeezed his shoulder. "He's probably just busy," she said.

When Ben visited at Christmas he asked if he'd had time to look at the paintings. "You're working through something with these landscapes," his father said. "It'll be interesting to see where it leads you."

Ben wanted to point out that his father was in hospice, that the chance was slim to none of him seeing anything beyond the New Year.

"I mean it'll be interesting to you, when you look back," his father said, and gave a short, dry laugh.

Erratic #57

Driving back to Chicago after the funeral, Ben told Mattie, "I guess that's the thing that hurt me most, that he didn't even say what was wrong with them."

"There's nothing wrong with them," she said moodily, staring out the passenger side window.

"Then why didn't he like them?"

She sighed and shifted in her seat. "You want things to be this or that," she said. "Sometimes you work on stuff that just isn't all that interesting to anybody but you. But you've still got to work on it, to get to the next place you need to go."

"Okay," Ben said, feeling more confused than hurt. "So why aren't my paintings interesting?"

Mattie turned and faced him. "I don't know," she said. "You have to answer that for yourself."

Erratic #70

After Mattie's graduation in June, she and Ben packed their belongings into a U-Haul truck and moved to Brooklyn. They spent the night at Ben's childhood home in Pennsylvania, with his father's widow and child. The next morning, they were barely on the interstate when Mattie said, "You seem fond of Emma."

Ben nodded. He liked his half-sister—it was hard not to. The little girl looked so much like his father, so much like him, and she talked constantly, in a way that might have been irritating but wasn't.

"She had a million questions, didn't she?" Ben said, slipping on his sunglasses.

"It was weird when that lady in the restaurant thought you were her father," Mattie said.

Ben fiddled with the dial on the radio. "Would you try to get NPR?"

Mattie reached for the dial and tuned to the station. "I think it tickled you," she said. After a minute of listening to music, she turned the radio down and said, "You could be, you know."

"I could be what?"

"Her father. You're the right age. A lot of people have kids at twenty-seven."

He nodded, unsure what Mattie was getting at. "Well, not me," he said.

"Not you," she agreed.

"She's a sweet kid," Ben said. "Did you hear the story she was telling me about the goat?"

Mattie said, "Uh-huh," and turned up the radio. "Mozart," she said. "I love Mozart."

Erratic #23

He got on at the Whole Foods at Columbus Circle, a long commute from their apartment in Sunset Park. Mattie got an under-the-table job as a photographer's assistant, and they negotiated studio space in an apartment that would've been tight for one person. But with Mattie often away at work in the evenings, Ben started enlarging some of the landscape photographs from his stash, gridding them out, and transferring them to large sheets of drawing paper.

For the first time in years, he really enjoyed what he was doing. The methodical routine of making the drawings seemed akin to constructing a wall. At the end of the night his hands were black with graphite and the paper worn with erasures, but he felt engaged with the forms emerging on the paper, block by block by block.

Erratic #62

She came to bed one night when he was already asleep, waking him by sliding her hands under his tee-shirt. They made love, quickly and without speaking, the wind hissing through the narrow gap where they'd left the window open.

She snuggled her head against his shoulder and immediately fell asleep. He lay awake for a long time remembering how, in Pennsylvania, he had lain in bed some nights and heard the geese making their migrations, honking to one another in the dark. They flew so low, he imagined he heard the beating of wings, and their cries reverberated inside his head long after they'd passed.

He went to sleep imagining himself a bird making the long flight without stopping, paying no attention to the night. He felt a tingle of fear at the blackness, plunging forward into the unseen world.

Erratic #109

Chicago friends who lived nearby started taking Mattie out to the museums and galleries on the weekend days he worked. Soon, on her days off, Mattie was hoofing her portfolio around. Mostly, she showed photos of the erratics that had been her senior thesis, but she'd re-processed the photos completely since graduation. From the photographer she worked for, she'd learned a few new techniques that enhanced the air of dreamy stillness surrounding the boulders.

Like a shoulder coming out of the earth, Ben said of one.

An abandoned emptiness, he said of another, that gabbro identified as part of the Canadian Shield.

An unproven certainty, he remarked of a third. He was hoping she'd take the hint, give the photographs titles, make them easier to digest.

She said, "An erratic is only an erratic because of its location." She flipped through several prints, then pushed one across the table to him. "The glacial ice was a mile thick at Chicago," she said. "This erratic is a kind of rock usually found in Wisconsin."

They were sitting at their table in Brooklyn, near the ocean they never thought about being close by. As Ben looked at the boulder, he could imagine the ice forming thick and white on the lake in Chicago, and the wind from Canada licking across it. They'd made many expeditions, when they lived in Chicago, all over the state, so Mattie could shoot these erratics.

He said, "You didn't even know what an erratic was until I told you. And for a long time, you kept calling them *eccentrics*."

She squinted at him as she laid down the photograph she'd been holding. "That's right," she said. She lifted her eyebrows. "And?" She indicated the photographs with her hands.

"Nothing," he said. "I just think it's interesting, that's all. Especially since you came from a place where there aren't any erratics." When she didn't say anything, he said, "Louisiana."

"Yeah, I know where I'm from." She rested her head lightly on the open fingers of her left hand and looked at him across the table. "Did I steal your idea?" she said. "Were you planning to photograph them?"

"You know I wasn't."

She nodded slightly. "Okay then," she said. She picked up another print and studied it. Then she put it down. "Where I came from doesn't matter," she said.

Erratic #3

It was January when Mattie left a message on Ben's phone while he was at work, telling him to call her back immediately. His first thought was that someone had broken into their apartment, but she answered with the news that she'd been signed by a gallery.

He tried to be happy for her, and he made himself sound happy. But he was the one with the M.F.A. He was the one who'd been the star at the 'tute. She'd won her share of praise, but she hadn't even been to graduate school yet, and even he could see that she still had things to learn about taking good photographs.

She asked him to come home so they could celebrate, but he was closing that night and wouldn't be home until after eleven. "Can't somebody cover for you?" she said. "This is important."

"I can't just walk out in the middle of a shift."

"You could if you were sick," she countered.

"But I'm not sick. And we're busy as crap on Friday nights."

So their Chicago friends took Mattie out to celebrate, with oysters and champagne. She came in around two, too tired to share the details.

Erratic #33

The landscape offers itself to her imagination, Ben thought, walking in the park during his lunch break, *in a way it does not offer itself to mine.*

Erratic #95

On a rare day when they were both free—pale March sunlight taking on a tinge of yellow, the first warm breath of spring in the air and the leaves barely a blush on the trees—they walked up to Prospect Park. They were just passing the band shell when Mattie turned to him and said, "There's no easy way to say this so I'll just say it. I'm moving in with Lex and Jennifer."

Ben nodded. The shock he felt was that he'd always thought if someone no longer loved him, he'd know immediately, by gut instinct. But nothing about Mattie had changed. They still slept together. She still looked the same—hadn't cut her hair, or made changes in her clothes. Her eyes were a little red, as if she might start crying. He stopped walking, and she stopped, so he squeezed her shoulder, pulled her in for a hug.

"It's all right," he said—reassuring himself, really, trying to think of what to do next, what would happen now.

"I'm not asking for your permission," she said.

Wounded, he said the first thing that came to mind: "What about the lease?"

She stopped in the middle of the sidewalk. She put her hands in her jacket pockets and looked away from him for a minute, at the empty concrete stage. He thought perhaps she hadn't considered the lease, so he pointed out that her name was on it.

She nodded, still not looking at him. "I'll pay my half of the rent until the lease is up, but I'm moving out at the end of the month."

"Okay," he said. "That's fine." At her look, he said, "Just saying."

They walked on in silence for a while longer, and then she stopped again and looked up at him, eyes dry and bright. "I can't believe that after living with me for three years, when I tell you I'm leaving you, your only concern is for the fucking lease."

"It's not my only concern."

Mattie had a temper, but her calmness was more frightening. She said, "Aren't you going to ask me what you've done wrong?"

"I haven't done anything," he said.

She nodded.

"You have your work," he said.

She looked at him sidelong. "And you're still trying to figure out how the inside wants to be solved."

He said, "If you don't want to live with me anymore, you should leave."

"I won't tell you that you'll thank me later," she said, and put her fingertips against his chin.

He took an involuntary step backwards. "Let's walk over to Seventh Avenue and get a cup of coffee. We can talk."

"Sure," she said, "that's much better than talking out here, where it's just you and me."

"Do you want to go home, then?"

She pushed her hand against his chest and twisted his sweatshirt in her clenched fist. "We don't have a home," she said.

He was surprised to see her tears.

Erratic #22

Erratics
Mattie Thibodeaux at Bonner-Hess Gallery
October 26–November 23, 2—

Erratic #14

When he walks through the door, the susurrus of voices washes over him. ". . . rocks left behind when the glaciers melted." "Stone birds in migration . . ." "One day you wake up, and you're the last of your kind." ". . . capturing something special and strange." "She says she doesn't know for sure why the stones attract her." "She mentioned Heidegger." "Nietzsche. I'm sure she said *Nietzsche*."

Erratic #48

Each is "erratic," with a number behind it: Erratic #48, Erratic #5, Erratic #22. She denies chronological order in her arrangement, though the reason is the first thing everyone asks.

"Which chronology?" she responds. "Geological? Or the order in which they were taken?"

Erratic #73

Boulders, some big as cars, shot in a dirt lot, in pastures, off the side of the highway. A few cluster on battlefields, where they served as good cover, or terrifying traps for men, their surfaces pocked from being struck by shrapnel, Minié balls.

Erratic #84

Mattie's in a bronze dress that hugs her everywhere, and high heels, though when she's barefoot, she's already five-nine. People cluster around her, and in her hand's a water bottle, not a wine glass. Black mascara's thick on her lashes. Blond hair swirls around her shoulders. Her fingernails are clean, knees and elbows moisturized. When she smiles, she flashes teeth so perfect, people can't help wondering if they're real. They're real, a product of summers on her grandfather's dairy farm, drinking tall glasses of milk with breakfast, lunch, and dinner. She's never had a cavity, and her bones are like iron.

She'll wear well, will not end as one of those stooped little women squinting through cigarette smoke, pink scalp showing through threads of hair, camera slung over her shoulder.

Erratic #8

Someone in the crowd mentions the Burren, where Mattie has never been, but she stands listening, lips slightly open, as the man weaves the story of Irish landscape, each stone in the field embodying the soul of a lost child.

"That's the first thing I thought of, looking at your photographs."

She asks if there are many lost children in Ireland, and he laughs and says, "Euphemism. Dead's what I'm saying," in that accent of his, charming, but even so, the little dart of displeasure stabs between her eyebrows.

"Well, I'm not Catholic," she says, meaning perhaps that the religious experience has somehow escaped her.

Erratic #79

A lone boulder in a field of long winter grass, bleached colorless in the unkind light. On the crowd's periphery, in front of this photograph, Ben stands, swilling down his third or fourth cup of sour white wine. Deep down, he always feared this, felt it like an ache in his bones predicting rain: Mattie, blooming late, existing in his periphery as he won the awards and fellowships, is the first to have a solo show. In Chelsea, no less. At quite a good gallery.

He works his jaw from side to side, studying the photograph. All those nights on the computer. She didn't even use film. He bites the inside of his lip, and when her mother comes alongside and takes his elbow, he turns and says, "Oh, hey, hey there. I wondered if you'd come up for the opening."

Loretta kisses him on the cheek and says, "Oh Ben, it's so lovely to see you," and shows her perfect teeth, her blue eyes crinkling. In a softer voice she says, "I'm so sorry things didn't work out."

"No, it's okay, really," he says.

She pats his arm.

Erratic #16

Loretta wouldn't have missed this for the world. Loretta tells people she is also an artist, painting, as she does, birdhouses, weathervanes, messages on rocks to be displayed in the garden: *Believe! Wonder! Smile!* She has her own line of note cards that she sells at her gift shop. She hands her business card to everyone she meets. Later, Ben will find one on the floor in the men's room.

While she talks, Ben thinks of all the times he's listened to Mattie's diatribes against her, spewing words like *uninformed, provincial, cloying*.

Even forming words in her heavy Southern drawl, Loretta's lips are fixed into a smile. She crinkles her eyes at him. She pats his arm again. She says, "Oh Ben, aren't you proud of her? Imagine! Our Mattie!"

Erratic #27

Mattie's in a rage, she has broken something, a cup, a glass, exactly what he doesn't remember. Maybe a camera. She kicks a chair across the room and screams, "Goddamn motherfucking piece of shit," and he looks up from the table where he's working on a drawing and then looks down again. His hands are trembling. Although they lived together, she was, he's pretty sure, never his Mattie.

Lex comes up and extends his hand. "Hey man, glad you could be here." Ben shakes his hand, says sincerely, "I wouldn't have missed it."

Erratic #43

This isn't my fault, he started to say, but then she turned and walked out of the apartment, and didn't come home until long past dark.

I was worried sick, he told her, and she said, *I'm sorry, I needed some space.*

Looking at the boulder in a field that seems to be somewhere south of Calumet, he wonders if she took the photo that particular summer afternoon, with the sun going down behind clouds. Around it, there's a lot of space.

Erratic #92

Although she does not shoot film, Mattie's photographs look as if they were taken with an old, not-very-good camera. She has manufactured light leaks, and the strange, bleached-out greens and blues of Kodachrome film from the sixties. Behind him, someone whispers *Amazing*, and Ben thinks, *yes, amazing is exactly the right word for it.* They are good photographs. They unsettle. They say something about loneliness, although for all the time they were together, he thought he was the lonely one. Mattie has a million friends.

Erratic #108

At the moment, Mattie's friends number about a hundred and sixty-three, and they spread out like a centrifugal force, with her at the center. Ben knows some of them, the old ones, the people she went to school with and the new ones from the neighborhood. They speak to him when their eyes meet his. One woman's cheeks redden and she looks at the floor and pretends not to see him.

"Hello, Jennifer," he says, forcing her to look up at him.

"Ben," she says, her voice frosty. She nods and moves on, Mattie's best friend, being loyal. Although Ben and Mattie are on friendly terms, Jennifer—never having loved him, or even liked him very much—has no need to let bygones be, to forgive or forget.

Erratic #7

There is nothing to forgive, unless Mattie has been making things up—not something Mattie's likely to do. She likes the truth too much, the ability to allow an unadorned fact or thing to speak for itself. All she has to do is capture it the right way, and figuring out what the right way is takes up most of her time.

Still, there's this one, the photograph he remembers her taking in the parking lot of their apartment building in Brooklyn. One hot Sunday morning in August, she lay on her belly on the concrete, fiddling with a photograph of a mackereled sky she'd pinned to the wooden fence with thumbtacks. In front of it, she placed a smooth white rock about as large as her fist. She spent an hour or so taking photographs, changing the focus, waiting for the sun to come out from behind the heavy clouds, waiting for the clouds to change the light.

When he chided her, saying she was cheating, she said, "Not at all. An erratic can be small as a pebble or as big as a house. This is a stone that's not where it's supposed to be. Therefore, an erratic."

If you look closely, you can see a thumbtack in the corner of the sky. He leans in and smiles, sharing this private joke, wondering what other illusions she's conjured.

The Grass Labyrinth

When my dad married Kerry, my mother said, "Well, Ben—there goes the house," as if Kerry might have married him for just this reason. And when, not quite three years into their unlikely marriage, my dad died, he did leave the house to Kerry. She lived there with their baby daughter. That my dad left the house to her didn't seem strange. I inherited the beach cottage in South Carolina—a whole bank account full of problems right there—and I had no use for a seventy-five-year-old fixer-upper in the middle of Pennsylvania. Though I was raised in the house, after my dad's funeral, I wasn't sure I'd ever have cause to go back, and the idea didn't trouble me.

But in June of the same year, my then-girlfriend Mattie and I moved from Chicago to Brooklyn and stayed overnight at the house, at Kerry's invitation. About eighteen months later, Kerry accepted an offer from the university library to buy my dad's papers. Mattie and I had broken up by then, and Kerry invited me for Thanksgiving, to look through the papers before the curator came to box everything up and remove it.

I knew the shape of my dad's studio. Shelf after shelf held boxes of old drawings; letters were things he scooped up a couple of times a year, crammed into file boxes without sorting, lugged up to the attic, and forgot about. Someone had told him once to save everything, and he obviously took the advice to heart. In her email, Kerry said she was relieved not to have to sort the important from the unimportant. "If you see something you want, you can take it," she wrote. "I've no idea what's here."

I knew it would take longer than Thanksgiving weekend to make even a stab at searching, but the prospect of spending the holiday alone in my grungy apartment was enough to make me accept Kerry's invitation. The woman I was casually dating at the time was going to her parents' house in Nebraska for the weekend. I dropped her at LaGuardia on Wednesday afternoon, then pointed my rusted-out truck toward I-80, headed across New Jersey and into Pennsylvania.

The afternoon was just shy of being one of those photographable late-autumn afternoons, kept from decorating a calendar only because most of the leaves had already fallen. Only a few deep mahogany shadows lay over the deciduous bands covering the hillsides, a palette of deep red, black, and gray, with a little white showing through from an early snowfall, patches of evergreens, and behind the mountains, nothing but blinding, pure cerulean. Driving along, I felt ridiculously proud to be from this beautiful place, as if I'd had a hand in designing it.

The previous summer, when Mattie and I drove this same road, she'd looked out at the landscape and said, "It's like a fucking postcard."

"You're just jealous," I'd said, "because you're from Louisiana," and she told me to fuck off but didn't deny what I'd said. I've seen that flat land dotted with drilling rigs and refineries, the white sky pinning everything under a layer of oppressive humidity. In this argument, Mattie didn't have a leg to stand on.

When I pulled up to the house, I saw immediately that it needed a paint job. My great-grandparents had it built from local stone, but the dark-gray wooden trim and windows were blistered and flaking. Since my last visit, Kerry had painted the old black front door sunflower yellow. On the porch steps, she'd arranged pumpkins and pots of chrysanthemums. When I was a kid, my mother gave up decorating for holidays. Every pumpkin got smashed, every string of Christmas lights disappeared. I wondered if the frat boys had given up these pastimes, or if Kerry just persisted despite them.

I rang the front bell and, when I got no answer, stepped off the porch and walked around my dad's studio to the back, to see if Kerry's car was in the driveway. It was, and down in the yard Kerry and Emma, rakes in hand, were piling leaves in a circle over the grass—Kerry with her hair in a messy bun, wearing green gardening clogs, faded jeans, and a brown sweater, and beside her Emma, in a flowered summer dress over a sweater and pink corduroys, with a red knit cap pulled down over her curls, and red mittens.

Maybe it was nervousness about the weekend ahead that kept me standing there watching them in silence, unmoving. I'd spent little time with them even before my dad died, and though I liked Kerry, she seemed a little distant.

"Well, what do you expect? She's younger than you, and she's your stepmother, for Christ's sake. I'd be distant, too, if I were in her place"—this from Mattie, who managed to be distant even though she stood, firmly, in her own place, which at the time was right beside me.

Emma and I had always gotten along great, and Kerry seemed pleased by my attempts to distract Emma when I visited in the autumn of my dad's last illness. When Kerry said, "Ben's your big brother," Emma invariably giggled and said, "No, he's not," though she was so young, I'm not sure she even understood what *brother* meant.

Emma's radar kicked in first, and when she turned and saw me standing in the driveway, she threw down her plastic rake. "Ben's here," she shouted at her mother, though Kerry had also seen me by then and was smiling, brushing her hair out of her face. Emma jumped up and down but made no move to come toward me, which seemed odd to me then. Now that I have children of my own, I understand a four-year-old's excitement as well as the natural reserve. Her mother told her I would be visiting for the holiday. She was excited for visitors, but after a year and a half, she had no idea who I was.

As Kerry cooked dinner that night, Emma and I sat on the couch while she "read" me her favorite books. Predictably, most of them had been written by our father, and since they'd been published long after I stopped reading picture books, they weren't engraved on my memory in the way they seemed engraved on hers. When I was in my twenties and people younger than I found out that Henry Tillman was my father, they'd inevitably go into rhapsodies about how one or another of his books had been their childhood favorite, how they could still recite the story by heart (and often they would do just that, no matter where we happened to be at the time), and how the illustrations had catapulted them into a magical place where the absurdity of being a child in an adult world seemed in focus for the first time. Then they'd get around to saying, "It must have been amazing to have him as a father." And when I'd shrug and say, "Yeah, I guess," they'd inevitably look disappointed— the failure to articulate mine, rather than reflecting in any way on him.

Emma was two when our dad died, and I can't imagine that she remembers much about him. Listening to her read the third book, I realized that the story she was reciting was about me, the summer after my folks divorced. The boy in the story—called Dan—decides to move out to the backyard. He sleeps on the tin roof of the garage, showers under the garden hose, eats vegetables from the garden and fruit from the trees. Occasionally, he goes into the house for a peanut-butter sandwich. All day, he occupies himself with building a dwelling in the hedge that separates his yard from the alley.

All's well until school begins. Dan has a tough time doing his homework in the underbrush. He has an even tougher time keeping his schoolbooks out of the rain. When the first snow comes, Dan looks at his bed of pine straw frozen in the thicket and then up at the bare apple trees. "Time to go in," he thinks, leaving open the possibility that when spring comes, he'll be back in his hedge, making his own place in the world.

When she finished reciting the book, Emma looked for a while at the last page—the boy standing in his old room—which was my old room, then Emma's. She asked if I thought Dan was a very silly boy for wanting to sleep in the yard.

"Not at all," I said. "One summer, I did that. In fact . . ." I turned back a few pages, where my father had made a full-page illustration of Dan's surprised face, which was my face at about age eight, "this boy is me."

Emma's brow furrowed. I was surprised how much she looked like my dad when she had that expression of trying to comprehend the incomprehensible. "Ben," she said patiently, "Dan is a little boy. You're not a little boy."

"Once upon a time I was." She still looked doubtful, so I said, "Look, my dad wrote this book about when I was little. Little like you are now."

Her face really clouded. "My papa made this book," she said, her bottom lip trembling.

"Emma," Kerry called from the kitchen, "I need you to set the table now. And Ben, would you open the wine?"

Kerry had made up the old daybed in my dad's studio for me, explaining that the guest room (once my mother's study) now had a quilting frame set up in the middle of it, quilting being her new hobby.

"I hope you don't mind," she said, smoothing a comforter over the foot of the bed, and I saw in her eyes that she, too, remembered the night she'd called me from this room, her voice ragged, my father's body cooling beside her.

"It's fine," I said, and I meant it. More nights than I can remember, I'd fallen asleep right here, listening to some new CD my dad wanted me to hear while he gridded out drawings at his work table. His hunched shoulders, the long ponytail bisecting his back, the smoke from his cigarette rising into the cone of lamplight, seemed the most solid things in the world after my mother left. I'd wake up the next morning and find him asleep at his work table, head pillowed on his arms, the drawing moved carefully to one side. Only now does it occur to me that maybe he needed my company as much as I needed his.

I lay in bed with the light out, looking out at the bare branches linked behind the window, illuminated by streetlight. In my dad's books, imagination quadrupled this grove of maples into a forest. Children got lost here. Animals lived out their anthropomorphic lives, far from the gaze of any human. Plenty of times I did my homework watching my dad sit at the window, sketchbook on his lap, smoking cigarettes and laying down washes of ink.

"Why don't you just work from photographs?" I used to ask him. "The view doesn't change all that much. A tree's a tree."

He'd give me one of his looks—the one that let me know I still had a lot to learn about art, and life as well—then pull down some book or magazine that featured paintings made from photographs.

"You see the difference?" he'd ask, and I'd say that I did, though I saw no difference. For years I made paintings from photographs, depicting people I didn't know, living lives that I never touched. Photographs aren't supposed to lie, but paintings are pure fiction. A painting of a photograph is a double lie, and for a long time, my whole shtick was this dig in the viewer's ribs.

As I lay in bed waiting for sleep to come, I heard Kerry moving around upstairs. Emma had fallen asleep on the couch, listening to us talk. Kerry carried her up to her room when we said our good nights, refusing my offer of help.

"I'm used to this," she said, and blushed, and I wondered if she was telling the truth about the quilt frame, or if she just didn't want me to come upstairs. She'd painted my grandmother's mahogany dining-room furniture a pale blue-gray, and replaced my mom's mini-blinds with lace tablecloths. Though I was intrigued by the audacity of the changes, I had my suspicions about what she might've done to the rest of the house.

The next morning—Thanksgiving—I woke to the smell of coffee and pancakes, and Emma standing over me in her red sleeper, wide-eyed.

"You snore," she said.

I thought, *How does a kid her age know about snoring? Where would she even learn the word for it?* And then I wondered if perhaps I wasn't the only man who'd spent the night in the house since my father died.

I carried that thought with me into the dining room, where Kerry had laid out a good breakfast on the gray-blue table—coffee and pancakes and orange juice, and even some vegan bacon she said tasted just like the real thing, though it didn't, not by a long shot.

I found myself watching her, wondering what her life had been in her widowhood. Kerry's not so much pretty as handsome, tall and big-boned, dark hair and eyes. At that age— she must have been twenty-seven then—her face looked smooth and untroubled, as if whatever pain she'd suffered had barely brushed the surface on its way to lodge deep inside, where it shone out through her eyes.

Only the eyes gave her away. My dad told me once that Kerry had a very old soul, and looking at her that morning, I saw what he meant. She was a young woman who'd lived a long life.

"If you're going to get through those papers, Ben, you need to get started," she said as she passed me the maple syrup. "Emma and I have some dinner plans up our sleeves, don't we, Emma?"

"Tanks-giving," Emma said, grimacing so that chewed pancakes pushed out between her teeth.

I looked outside. The day was, if possible, even more beautiful than the previous day—cloudless blue sky, gray trees, the charge of a sharp chill in the air visible in its clarity.

"No time to go out and play?" I asked.

Kerry smiled. "No time," she said.

Emma was watching us, fork poised in her right fist. "How about this?" she said. "We do our work, then go outside."

"Emma," I said. "What a brilliant idea."

"Thank you," she said, and I remembered—or maybe this is where I learned—that irony is lost on children. What you tell them is what they believe.

Kerry said she hadn't touched my father's papers—"Couldn't bear to," she said—and for proof, dust covered the archival boxes that held his drawings. He worked for twenty-five years as a writer and illustrator, and the boxes were, as I'd expected, full of sketches, ink and pencil drawings, watercolors, pastels. After his first book—*A Rabbit with a Habit*, a silly watercolor romp starring a klepto-bunny and the boy who's his accomplice—he mostly worked in pastels. Sitting on the floor in the studio with a box of these spread out around me, I marveled at the depth of color and the richness of the palette. These were drawings that had never made it into his books, and some of them were exquisite.

And then I started digging back to the oldest work. These were works on paper that—judging by the dates—he must have done at Tyler and in the five or so years after.

"I didn't start out to be an illustrator," he used to tell me. "It's just where I ended up."

I remembered this while I was looking at his old work. I understood that basically, working from photos of strangers taken from websites, all I was doing was illustrating other people's lives—picking up a story in the middle, rendering it in oils, and hanging it on the wall as a testament to my skills of execution and appropriation. All that was missing was the accompanying narrative, and the context supplied that so well, and so tritely, that words weren't even necessary.

Somehow I'd managed to get two degrees in art without understanding this. I felt like the dig in the ribs had suddenly been reversed. We all have our ah-ha moments, and this was mine.

Why did comparing my dad's old paintings to his illustrations show me this? It's not that his paintings were superior. Just the opposite, in fact: The illustrations were superb. His paintings never got at anything—the internal logic derived from the melding of form, paint, and the mind of the artist, where was that? Had I even known to look for it in my own work? Absolutely not. When people called my paintings *clever*, I'd taken this for a compliment.

"How's it going?" Kerry asked. I turned, and she was leaning on the doorframe holding a dishtowel, watching me; I had the feeling she'd been standing there for a while.

I didn't trust myself to speak. She nodded and said, "I made us some tea. You've been in here for hours."

She and I sat at the dining table, blue mugs of some herbal blend in front of us, me with my back to the large window overlooking the back yard. Cool gray shadows were beginning to gather in the corners of the room; in maybe an hour, we'd need lights. A pie in the oven was making the house smell good, but for a Thanksgiving, the kitchen seemed oddly at rest.

"It doesn't take long to cook a mushroom tart," Kerry said, when I remarked on this, and I realized that I'd been expecting a turkey though I knew she and Emma were vegetarian.

"Where's Emma?" I said.

Kerry nodded toward the window. "In the back yard, playing." She smiled. "Yes, she finished her work. She scooped the seeds out of the squash and stirred the cranberry sauce while it was cooking."

I turned and looked outside. Emma was raking more leaves into the pile she and Kerry made the day before. "If you want," I said, "I'll be happy to bag up those leaves before I go."

"Ah, no, no, no," Kerry said, and leaned forward, her eyes bright. "Emma and I are building a labyrinth. This is step one."

"Killing the grass?"

Kerry explained that she'd put a layer of black plastic under the leaves, which would compost over the winter. In spring, she'd remove the black plastic and dig the fresh compost into the newly bared earth.

I was surprised how much the whole idea disturbed me—not the labyrinth per se but that she'd planned a major overhaul of the space on her own.

I said, "You know, a lot of people associate that yard with my dad's books. It was the whole mysterious universe to them. Just looking at those illustrations again . . ." I nodded toward his studio, "I think he couldn't have made up those stories without having the back yard to set them in."

Kerry nodded, but she didn't say anything. She held her mug between her hands, and I noticed that she'd stopped wearing her wedding ring.

"Who'll help you build this maze?" I said.

"Emma," she said.

"Oh, right," I said. "Emma."

She lifted her eyebrows and looked away, while a corner of her mouth quirked. I've come to know this expression as saying far more than words; it's the face she makes when argument is useless, when the other person's not ready to hear.

"Why do you want a maze anyway?" I said.

"It's not a maze, it's a labyrinth," she said. "A maze is a game, full of trick turns and dead ends. The whole point of going into a maze is finding your way out again. A labyrinth is just a spiral winding inward."

"And the point is . . ." I gestured, urging her on.

She smiled. "There is no point," she said.

"Then why tear up the yard?"

"Is that what you think I'm doing?"

When I didn't say anything, she surprised me by reaching over and taking hold of my wrist. "Come outside with me," she said.

We crossed the driveway and walked down the three stone steps to the lower yard, where Emma was still at work with her rake. "A lab rat, a lab rat, we're building a lab rat," she shouted when she saw us.

"What's a lab rat, Emma?" I said, crouching so we were eye-to-eye. She smelled like hot pennies and dirt when she hugged me.

"You know," she said, and drew a spiral in the air with her finger.

I picked Emma up and carried her around the yard while Kerry explained her plans. Her vision mostly involved the small square of lawn. I was relieved when she gestured to the overgrown borders where rhododendron, forsythia, roses, and winterberry jumbled among the ferns, blackened now after the frost, and said that they wouldn't be part of this project. As the neighbors' back yards became more manicured, ours had grown wilder. The neighbors added brick patios, stone fountains, wooden decks, perennial beds, while my dad seemed intent on cultivating underbrush, and that cultivation has been completely successful.

Kerry planned to make the walls of the labyrinth out of tall grasses, and the path from gravel. "Sometimes, you'll have a bench or a statue or even a fountain at the center of the labyrinth," she said.

"What's at the center of this one?" I said.

She smiled. "We'll have to wait to find out," she said.

As the three of us made dinner—I had salad and bread-slicing duty, while she made the mushroom tart and the stuffed squash and Emma snapped the green beans—Kerry explained how she'd gotten the idea to build a labyrinth from a sculpture garden she and my dad had once visited.

"It was a really crappy little labyrinth," she said, sipping at her glass of wine. "Mostly overgrown, and the grasses had been taken over by weeds, but I thought, I could do something like that and make it really nice."

"What did my dad say?"

"Oh," she said, and looked at me sidelong. "You know how he was."

"Not really."

She gave me a skeptical look and did a pitch-perfect imitation of my dad. "*We don't need a labyrinth, Kerry. Besides, it's too much work. And who'll maintain it? You can't just build a labyrinth and then let it go.*"

I nodded. "I have to say . . . I agree with him."

"We . . . are getting . . . a lab rat," Emma intoned into her bowl of beans. She grinned at me. "Ben, will you help Mama and me make our lab rat?"

"Never!" I said, and she laughed. I wiggled my fingers at her in a mousey way. "Never, never, never!!"

By now, both she and Kerry were laughing. "I'm serious," I said to Kerry.

"So am I," she said, smiling.

"This is going to be way more work than you think it is," I said.

She popped one of Emma's snapped beans into her mouth. "We'll see about that," she said.

"Yeah," Emma said. "We'll see about that."

Our last Thanksgiving together, Mattie and I attended a rooftop celebration in our Brooklyn neighborhood, well-stocked with Molson's and our hipster friends. The turkey dinner was ultimate camp: instant mashed potatoes, frozen peas, dressing out of a box, a turkey roll, cranberry sauce that still retained the shape of the can, and sweet potatoes laden with marshmallows. We laughed that this was just like Granny used to make, though my grandmother died when I was four, and I don't remember her meals. Back at home that night, Mattie said she'd had a great time, and I wondered if we'd attended the same party.

The meal at Kerry's was simple. Except for the cranberry sauce and pumpkin pie, nothing marked it as being different from the usual meals she prepared. Between the two of us, we did drink two bottles of pinot noir; I woke in the pre-dawn hours, unable to fall back to sleep. Red wine does that to me.

I thought about turning on the light and getting back to sorting papers, but that seemed better done after coffee and a good night's sleep.

Instead, I thought about that damned labyrinth. It was mostly what we'd talked about over dinner. Why, I'd asked, make a labyrinth out of grass? Shouldn't the dividers between the windings of the paths at least have some substance? I could envision the mess—grass flopping into gravel, the whole thing disintegrating into an eyesore. We get a lot of snow here. How was she planning to keep the gravel on the path and out of the beds of grass? I suggested box hedge, or even stone, for the walls. When pressed, I admitted that my idea came mostly from the maze in *The Shining*—tall and impenetrable.

Kerry laughed. "Let's keep it simple," she said. "I just want a place to do my walking meditation."

"If that's what you want," I said, "why don't you just walk in circles around the back yard?"

"I do that now," she said. "But a labyrinth gives a space a kind of order that's very peaceful."

"It gives you a destination," I suggested. "Which you said earlier was not the point."

She thought about this for a minute. "I think," she said slowly, "it's more about measuring time. It's about centering yourself in a place. There's some comfort in just knowing the place is there. You carry it with you, but it's also a real, physical place." After a long pause, she started to speak, then fell silent again.

"What?" I prompted, genuinely curious. Kerry and I had mostly talked about pragmatics in the past—what the hospice nurses were doing to relieve my dad's pain, did I want some of his art books and if so, should she keep them for me, or did I want her to mail them (*keep them*, I said, which turned out to be the wise decision—they remain on the shelves).

"Well," she said, "I was going to say, it's like when you care for someone, and that person is away. You miss them, but you still carry the warmth inside you of being in the relationship. It's very different from just being alone."

I laughed. "Who are we talking about here? You or me?"

She looked surprised. "The human race, I think."

"I'm not following this. You mean you want to have a labyrinth because it's like being in a relationship with someone who isn't there?"

"Not at all. It's more like . . . walking meditation is being able to love. Having the labyrinth is being able to love, and also loving someone in particular." She smiled at me, and shook her head. "I think we've had way too much wine. I know I have."

Still mulling this conversation over, I got dressed, put on my shoes and jacket, and went out the back door, thinking I'd pay some last respects to my childhood refuge. Summers, I'm sure I spent more time in that yard than in the house, and even when the weather turned cold, I'd pretend to be a soldier weathering the icy hardships of the forests not yet claimed by William Penn.

When I went out, I saw Kerry at the bottom of the three stone steps, her back to the house, looking out at the yard. She wore a down jacket over her nightgown, and boots, and hugged herself against the chill. It was cold—probably in the mid-twenties—and daylight still a couple hours away. The wind had picked up during the night, and the fallen leaves rustled against each other inside the circle in the grass where Emma and Kerry had piled them.

What I did next, I can't explain except as a response to being out in the dark and the cold with a woman I was fond of. As I came up behind her, I said her name quietly, and when she turned, I embraced her. I like to believe there was nothing sexual in my touch or in my intention, that I'd have done the same had it been Emma or my mother standing there instead.

Maybe what Kerry responded to was simply another warm body. She's never said what she was thinking when she pulled me close and laid her head on my shoulder. The gesture seemed one of weariness, almost resignation—she was tired and cold, and here was someone to shore her up.

Even as we stood motionless, holding one another, I started to fear what would happen when standing motionless became awkward, as it surely would soon. I'd initiated the touch, so was it up to me to decide what happened next? Kerry had some say in this as well. I wondered what she'd do, if I let my arms drop and took a half-step back. I wondered what she'd do, if I kissed her. And then I wondered what Henry would have done in this situation.

Well, I knew. He'd never have touched this woman unless he wanted her, and once he'd made that decision, he'd have held on as if his life depended on it. He would not have wimped out in the middle of a hug.

Then I felt someone tugging at the hem of my coat, and Kerry stepped swiftly away, allowing Emma to move between us: Emma, in her fluffy rabbit bedroom slippers and fleece sleeper. "I woke up," she said. As Kerry lifted her, Emma said, "I went to your room and you weren't there."

"She's a bit of a sleepwalker," Kerry murmured, brushing Emma's hair with her hand. The three of us huddled in a circle, Kerry with her cheek pressed against the top of Emma's head.

As Emma nestled against her mother's shoulder, she turned toward me. Her eyes grew wide, as if she were seeing me for the first time. "Did Papa come back?" she asked Kerry.

"It's Ben, sweetie," Kerry said. She patted Emma's back. "Let's get you inside. It's cold out here."

Emma's eyes closed, but she reached out her hand to me. "You come too," she said. As if trying the words on inside her mouth before she released them, she said, "Papa. Ben. Papa Ben."

I went back inside too wired to sleep. By the time Kerry came downstairs at eight-thirty, I'd been working in the studio for a couple of hours, halfway through a pot of coffee. Kerry seemed grave, I thought, as she said good morning, and closed the glass-paned doors behind her. Her hair hung loose over her shoulders. Her eyes, though bleary, seemed calm. She sat at my dad's work table, facing me.

"Emma will be awake any minute, so I don't have time to finesse my way into this," she said. "People come together for all sorts of reasons, in all kinds of ways. When Henry and I got together, a lot of people thought we were both crazy. Including you, probably."

I opened my mouth to speak, but she held up her hand. "Henry and I understood one another. Sometimes we didn't need to talk, and other times, we talked like maniacs. I loved him, and I made sure the time we had together was good.

"But that was another part of my life, with someone who just happened to be your father. Anywhere else in the world, Ben, you and I are just two people. And as I'm sure must be obvious to you by now, I don't give a damn what other people think."

"Yes," I said.

"I just want to say, you mean a lot to Emma and me. I'd really like it if you helped us work on the labyrinth."

That wasn't exactly what I'd been expecting her to say, though if I had to say what I was expecting, I'd have trouble articulating it. So I said, "Well, how about Christmas?"

She smiled. "Not a great time for landscaping here in Pennsylvania."

"Maybe not," I said.

"Besides, Emma and I are spending the holidays with my sister in Minneapolis."

"She came to the funeral," I said. "I liked her."

Kerry nodded. She was rubbing the hem of her sweater between her thumbs, and watching what she was doing. After a while, she said, "You've got a lot to do. A lot of choices to make."

I looked around at the boxes of illustrations open on the floor around me. I'd set aside a few to take back. "I'm not nearly finished with this," I said.

"No rush."

I said, "Well, the curator . . ." and she said, "There's no firm deadline." She looked up at me. "You take your time. And when spring comes, if you want to work on the labyrinth, I'd like that. I know Emma would too."

"I've been conscripted," I said.

"Nope," she said. "It's strictly a volunteer force."

"Maybe by spring, I'll be finished with the papers."

She smiled. "We'll see."

Then Emma's face appeared, pressed against the glass, her nose and lips flattened, her fingers wiggling at either side of her face.

"Oh no, it's the lab rat," I called out.

Still in her sleeper and rabbit slippers, Emma opened the door with a flourish. "Papaben, papaben, papaben," she sang, dancing into the room. "It's really just your little girl."

Provenance

Kerry employs cast-offs in her garden. A wood-framed window eight feet tall, flaking white paint and missing its glass, supports a New Dawn rambler. Pansies spill from the old porcelain pedestal sink that leaked in the upstairs bath, and now ferns circle the white columnar base. The neighbors still haven't spotted the solid oak door they tossed during a renovation. Painted periwinkle and wreathed in clematis, the door stands like a rectangle of sky between lush hemlocks, allowing passage out to the alley.

Why does she do these things? Kerry herself wonders at times, while she's fixing an old brass key onto the Sally Holmes rose, or tying a flour sifter into the hemlock's boughs. From her perch on a high branch in the middle of some act of decoration, she's looked down into the labyrinth at the center of the back yard, and asked herself why that elaborate construction wasn't enough. Why must she keep adding to it?

This morning Kerry sits on the top step of her back porch, holding a china saucer onto which she's Super-Glued a china teacup. She's weighing an idea, testing it against an aesthetic ideal: Would the hard, flower-patterned china contrast nicely with the deep blue fruit of the nannyberry viburnum?

Though it's late summer, she envisions the rose-painted cup with snow mounded above the lip like meringue. Freezing and thawing are bound to crack the china. She turns the saucer upside-down, the cup hanging bell-like from its center. Positioning it this way might spare the cup, but she started out to make an elevated puddle for the birds, so they might drink without the cats pouncing on them. Kerry has three cats that lurk under the hedges, dash inside with prey dangling from their mouths, strew the yard with feathers and an occasional beak. Upside down, the cup and saucer become a perch, at best.

"Ben, do you think . . ." she calls over her shoulder to her husband, who's in the kitchen making a snack for their younger daughter.

"Just a minute," he says. When he comes to the screen door, Jane's riding his hip. Barefoot, in a tee-shirt and diaper, she's sucking half an orange.

Kerry explains her plan for the cup and saucer, ending with, "Is this a lame idea?"

He sits beside her on the step, settling the toddler between them. He says, "Birds don't expect to find a puddle in a tree. They might not know what to do with it."

She watches him, glad that he doesn't dismiss her ideas reflexively. She says, "I've seen them drink rain out of gutters."

He concedes her point. Then he adds, "The viburnum isn't tall. If cold's all you're worried about, you could always take the cup out before winter, and put it back in spring."

Though this contradicts her plan, she punches him lightly on the bicep. "Brilliant," she says. She leans across Jane and kisses him. He seems tired this morning, distracted—his painting, she knows, is not going well. He's worked his way into a dead end, and though he can see the problem, has no idea how to solve it. She's seen these fallow times come and go. Yet each time he hits a wall, Ben responds as if it's never happened: He can't sleep. He talks of little but how he shouldn't even call himself a painter, or else doesn't talk at all. He doesn't believe her when she tells him the hard time will pass, yells at her to stop being so fucking condescending.

They sit quietly, looking out at the grass labyrinth that takes up most of their small back yard. At its center, there's no room for a meditation bench or even a chair, so it's marked with a stone rabbit Kerry pulled out of somebody's trash. The first time he saw the rabbit, Ben thought she'd put it there as a joke.

In all the years they've been together, Ben can count the times he's walked the gravel path. Whimsy grates on his aesthetic, and the rabbit's definitely whimsical, made of some cheap composite meant to resemble stone. If asking wouldn't hurt her feelings, he'd ask Kerry to remove it, but she's under the impression gimcrackery exudes charm.

The hemlock hedge he played in as a child is larded with gnomes and bric-a-brac, some of it worse than this teacup she's epoxied to a chipped and unmatched saucer. When Kerry flips the saucer upside down, testing the adhesion, Jane reaches fingers sticky with orange juice to stroke the treasure.

Kerry gives it away, though Ben warns, "She'll break it."

"It's okay," Kerry murmurs. Ben doesn't know if she means *so what if the junk gets broken*, or *don't worry because Jane's got a steady hand.* He doesn't ask, just shifts his gaze from his wife and daughter into the labyrinth.

At the center of the spiral, the rabbit rests on its haunches, ears erect, front paws together in an attitude of prayer. According to the creator of this kitsch, animals pray to a god, subscribe to a religion in which prayer is the means of communication. What they pray for, beyond food and a chance to live another hour, Ben doesn't even want to imagine.

As he sits looking out at the rabbit, Ben wonders why he's never offered to make something to replace it.

I don't do it because I'm an artist, he tells himself, *not a landscape designer.* In the next moment, he chides himself for even thinking this way. Plenty of artists would have built a decent sculpture for the garden, just because they'd like something better to look at than a composite-stone rabbit. He hasn't replaced the rabbit because he's never considered it until now. The backyard is Kerry's domain. If she wants to hang the dining-room chairs from the power lines, that's her business.

When Jane drops the cup and saucer onto the stone step, the handle breaks, and a chip flies off the lip of the saucer. He leans over and kisses her on top of the head, then stands and stretches.

"Going to work," he says, and as he turns to go inside, he hears Kerry tell the child, "A cup without a handle can still hold water."

Ben charcoals diamond shapes across the paper thumbtacked to the wall. All he wants is for his hand to move, for his arms to feel the pull of putting lines on paper. It's muscular, a reflex. He's not thinking about diamonds. He's thinking about the texture of fur and the smell of oranges and the sound the charcoal makes as it rasps across the paper.

Some of the shapes look like kites, some like featureless faces. Over and over his hand moves, left to right, filling the page as if he's writing in a special alphabet that has only one character, a language in which meaning is derived from variations in the width of the body, the intersection of lines.

He used to paint people, then landscapes.

He gestures widely, and the charcoal skips off the paper and onto the wall. He brings it back to the margin. When he gets to the bottom of the page, he goes back to the top and begins again, laying shape over shape over shape.

He does this for hours. Muscle memory. His hands black with charcoal keep moving, moving, moving.

Drawing comes out of the body.

He will work for as long as he can.

Stories and essays by Charlotte Holmes have appeared in *Epoch, New Letters, Antioch Review*, and *The Sun*. She is author of *Gifts and Other Stories*. Born in Augusta, Georgia, Holmes received an M.F.A. from Columbia University and was a Stegner fellow at Stanford. She teaches at Pennsylvania State University.